NORTHWESTERN UNIVERSITY PRESS

MEDIEVAL FRENCH TEXTS

GENERAL EDITOR

NORMAN B. SPECTOR,

NORTHWESTERN UNIVERSITY

THE TALE OF BALAIN

VIR·O·VNO

The Tale of Balain

FROM *THE ROMANCE OF THE GRAIL,*

A 13TH CENTURY FRENCH PROSE ROMANCE

TRANSLATED FROM THE OLD FRENCH

BY DAVID E. CAMPBELL

NORTHWESTERN UNIVERSITY PRESS

EVANSTON

1972

David E. Campbell is Assistant Professor of French at Northwestern University and a member of the Committee on Medieval Studies there.

The frontispiece is from the British Museum, Harley MS no. 2904, Folio 4, and is reproduced by courtesy of the Trustees of the British Museum.

Copyright © 1972 by Northwestern University Press
Library of Congress Catalog Card Number: 72–77830
ISBN 0–8101–0385–0
Printed in the United States of America

FOR EUGÈNE

CONTENTS

A need for reliable editions and translations of some of the masterpieces of Old French literature, especially those that are of major interest to students of English, has been felt for some time. The study of Western literature, and in particular English poetry and prose, has been seriously hampered by the unavailability of important medieval French texts to students and teachers who are not trained in the old language.

The Northwestern University Press Medieval French Texts have come into being to fill this troublesome gap. With *The Tale of Balain* the press launches a series of translations of works in medieval French literature that will make possible more direct access to a treasury of hitherto little known authors, genres, and literary traditions. The Balain story is a fitting one with which to begin this series. It will be welcomed by all those interested in Arthurian romance and the Grail story. An edition of *The Tale of Balain* in the original medieval French, edited by David E. Campbell, will be published shortly by Northwestern University Press as a companion volume to this one.

NORMAN B. SPECTOR

Introduction

ALTHOUGH THE TALES OF KING ARTHUR AND HIS Knights of the Round Table are known throughout the English-speaking world, they are usually known not in their earlier forms but in versions such as those written by Alfred Tennyson, Algernon Swinburne, Mark Twain, and more recent writers such as T. H. White, Walt Disney, and J. R. R. Tolkien. It is a testimony to the fascinating qualities of these tales that they have captivated the imagination for the last eight centuries; but it would be a pity if our fascination with the vitality of the "matter of Britain" caused us to deny ourselves the great pleasure of reading the tales in their original form. It was with this end in mind — to acquaint the larger public with that pleasing exercise—that this translation of *The Tale of Balain* was undertaken.

Two manuscripts are known of the *Balain* section of the thirteenth-century French romance called the *Continuation of the Merlin*. The two manuscripts are in England: one in the British Museum (Add. 38117), the other at the Cambridge University Library (Add. 7071). The British Museum, or so-called "Huth," manuscript was first published in 1886 by Gaston Paris and Jacob Ulrich. A two-volume work entitled *Merlin,* it was part of the series of the Société des Anciens Textes Français. It was published again in 1942 by Dominica Legge in the University of Manchester French Classics series with the title *Le Roman de Balain*. In 1945, when the manuscript which is now in the Cambridge University Library was found, it became apparent that a new critical edition of the text was needed because of the extent of omissions from the Huth Manuscript brought to light by the Cambridge Manuscript.[1] Such an edition is now in

---

1. For the details of the discovery see Eugène Vinaver, ed., *The Works of Sir Thomas Malory* (New York: Oxford University Press, 1954), III, 1279ff.

preparation, and my translation is based upon this newly established critical text.

The vast cyclic romances of the thirteenth century have been hidden from our view until quite recently by the lack of reliable or accessible editions. The reason for there having been so few such editions is not so much that the works are enormous in size as that they are formally quite complex. Fanni Bogdanow has demonstrated that the *Continuation of the Merlin* is part of a much longer and more complex cyclic romance, composed probably between 1230 and 1240 A.D. and known far and wide across Europe as *The Romance of the Grail.*[2] This romance included *The Story of the Holy Grail* and the story of Merlin (based on Robert de Boron's late twelfth-century poem), with its continuations, *The Quest of the Holy Grail* and *The Death of Arthur. The Romance of the Grail* formed an aesthetic whole which was not recognized as such until Miss Bogdanow had succeeded in placing it in the context of medieval fiction. She has shown it to be a later version of another cyclic romance, also many hundreds of pages long, which is known as the "Vulgate" version of the Arthurian romances. This earlier romance, probably composed between 1220 and 1225, was built around a prose romance whose central character was Lancelot. The emphasis in *The Romance of the Grail* is, however, not on Lancelot, but on the story of the rise and fall of Arthur and his kingdom, the *royaume aventureux;* here the role of the Lancelot story is considerably reduced, and it is Arthur who plays the role of "hero." What the author is concerned with is the fate of

2. Miss Bogdanow has reconstructed the cycle in her book *The Romance of the Grail* (Manchester: Manchester University Press, 1960). There are also two Spanish printed versions of *El Baladro del Sabio Merlin* (cf. Bogdanow, *The Romance of the Grail,* pp. 271ff.).

Arthur's kingdom, jeopardized by Balain's dolorous stroke, redeemed for a time by Galahad, and brought to a tragic conclusion by the feud between Lancelot and Gawain.

None of this, however, is told in a straightforward manner, and the unfortunate aspect of the situation is that one cannot appreciate the majestic power of the cyclic structure of *The Romance of the Grail* unless he reads it all. The first part of the cycle, *The Story of the Holy Grail,* is the story of that mysterious vessel or bowl which is the object of the quest in subsequent adventures. *Merlin* and the *Continuation of the Merlin* tell the tale of the foundation and the early years of Arthur's kingdom, when Balain's dolorous stroke lays waste the land. The quest episode tells about the arrival of Galahad, the Good Knight, who heals all, breaks the spell cast on the land by Balain's ill-fated presence, and puts an end to suffering by achieving the Grail Quest. The *Death of Arthur* gives an account of the tragic events leading up to the downfall of the kingdom and of the subsequent fate of the kingdom of Logres.

Although the events in any one of the tales contained in this composition overlap, the whole forms a unit, thematically balanced between *The Tale of Balain* and *The Quest of the Holy Grail.* The function of *The Tale of Balain* is two-fold. It serves to pick up threads of narrative previously partially developed and then dropped and to prepare what is to follow. I have translated the text in full, including the long passage which Miss Legge omitted from her 1942 Manchester edition. The passage begins on Folio 112[b] of the Huth manuscript with the sentence: "'Rois,' fait Merlins, 'or laissiés ceste parole a tant; assés l'avés dit.'"[3] and

---

3. "'King,' said Merlin, 'leave this matter as it is; you've said enough about it.'"

ends on Folio 123^d with: "Et li rois dit que che veult il moult bien"[4] (pp. 33–59 in this translation).

Here is a brief summary of the episode: Merlin announces to the king that he is going to have to fight two fearsome enemies, Rion's brother Nero and his own brother-in-law King Lot of Orkney, who thinks his son Mordred was drowned at Arthur's command with the other children born on May Day. Arthur gets ready for battle. Balain and Balaan [Balain's brother] learn from a hermit that there is going to be a great battle between Arthur and Nero. They see Arthur's people, who are fewer in number, have several successes, then begin to weaken. The two brothers enter the battle and perform prodigious feats. Arthur, Kay, and Hernil de Rivel act with great prowess, but no one does nearly as much as Balain, the Knight with the Two Swords. Arthur says that Balain must be not an ordinary knight but a supernatural being. Merlin goes to find Lot and tries to turn him back by telling him that Mordred isn't dead. Lot, however, doesn't want to listen, so Merlin announces Lot's approach to the king. Arthur's barons, notably Pellinor, encourage him. The two armies come together with great violence. Lot, after accomplishing deeds of marvelous prowess, unhorses Arthur, but is killed by Pellinor. The men of Orkney are put to rout. Later, Gawain, son of Lot, will kill Pellinor and his three sons, Perceval's brothers, for revenge.

King Arthur has the dead buried. At Lot's funeral Gawain, then only eleven, swears to avenge him. Victor over twelve kings, Arthur has their statues placed on top of a tower in such a way that they bow to his. Then he holds a great feast. Merlin casts a spell which causes the candles held by the statues to burn perpetually until the day he [it is not clear in the text

4. "And the king said that he was quite agreeable to this."

to whom the author is referring here] dies through the trickery of a woman, and until that time when the Knight with the Two Swords will strike the dolorous stroke which will cause the beginning in Great Britain of an amazing pain and pestilence that will last twenty-two years.

In addition to the many obvious references in this section to past and future events, to disappearing and reappearing characters and themes, the central plot, Arthur's conflict with Nero and Lot, identifies the episode as an element in the structure of *The Romance of the Grail* as a whole. The motivation of this conflict can only be understood in the light of episodes occurring many pages earlier and separated from it by many intervening episodes. Since the passage interrupts *The Tale of Balain* and the tragic race toward catastrophe, it integrates that tale into the whole structure by causing the reader's mind to encompass it as he recalls the events that led up to it and anticipates those that will result. As examples of the many events and characters which compose the fabric of the *Merlin,* let us consider two: first, the role of two characters, Morgan and Rion; and, next, a major episode, the battle between Nero, Lot, and Arthur, its motivation and results.

Long before the beginning of our text on Folio 94^c of the Huth manuscript, after Arthur has retrieved his sword Escalibor from the mysterious hand in the lake, the text says that Merlin speaks of the magical qualities of the scabbard and then "...ains atent ceste chose a conter dusques a cele eure que l'istoire le devise, comment Morgue sa seur li embla pour baillier a son ami que au roi Artu se devoir combatre."[5] We hear nothing further of the matter until the

5. "...so this matter will wait to be told about until the time when the tale tells it, how Morgan, his sister, took it from him to give to her lover who had to fight with King Arthur."

present episode of *The Tale of Balain* on Folio 120ᵇ(sixty-four pages in print), where Merlin counsels Arthur to guard the scabbard of his sword carefully,[6] and it is in the text immediately following (through Folio 122ᵈ) that Morgan's treacherous gift of the scabbard to her lover is told. In this way a link is established between an episode within the central section of *The Tale of Balain* and one in an earlier section of the *Merlin*. The intervening space is twenty-six folios, or about sixty-five printed pages.

The second example is the establishment of the motives for the great battle between Nero, Lot, and Arthur (Folios 112ᵇ to 123ᵈ of the Huth manuscript). At Folio 95ᶜ a certain King Rion of North Wales sends word to Arthur that he demands his homage and his beard to put with that of eleven other kings he has already conquered. Arthur refuses and says that he will have to take him by force—this by the middle of the second column, Folio 96ᵃ. On Folio 97ᵇ King Lot's wife is delivered of a son, whom they baptize Mordred and send off to Arthur, as they have been commanded. The ship that carries the child is wrecked, and only the child survives. He is found and taken to Nabur le Desrée, who raises him with his son Sagremor. In the meantime, Arthur, in order to foil a prophecy that he would be killed by a boy born on May Day, plans to kill all infants born on that day. But he decides instead to set them afloat in a boat without a pilot. They are found and rescued by Oriant, the father of Acanor, and are lodged in a castle called the "Châtel aux Genvres." The barons of Arthur's realm are indignant about

---

6. "Le Fuerre de votre espee gardés bien, que je vous di bien que vous ne trouverés ja mais si merveilleuse si vous la perdés." ["Take good care of your scabbard, for I say to you truly that if you lose it you'll never find another one that's as marvelous."]

the treatment meted out to their children, but Merlin explains why it was necessary, and they are appeased. The episode ends in the middle of Folio 99ᵃ, where the tale of Balain begins.

We are in the presence here of two themes which are distinct from each other, yet related in a certain way. The first deals with Arthur's rejection of Rion's demands and occupies only half a folio. The second is the supposed drowning of Lot's son. The transition from the first to the second is abrupt; there is no apparent causal connection between them. The second theme extends from Folio 96ᵃ to the middle of 99ᵃ. We then follow the adventures of Balain and hear no more of these two incidents until Folio 112ᵇ, when Merlin announces that Nero, Rion's brother, and Lot are about to attack Arthur. If the first letters of the characters' names were used as sigla, the sequence would look like this: R - L - B - R - L. Rion's cause for grievance is presented first, and his army is dealt with first; Lot's tragedy is presented second, and his defeat follows Rion's. The resolution of the problems is presented in the same order as the original statement of each: the two parts are separated by a long account of Balain's adventures.

That this is not simply an unusual coincidence is shown by the fact that the arrangement is quite symmetrical. After the battle with Lot the king asks: "Where are Balain and Balaan?" And Merlin answers that they have left. The matter is then dropped so that the author can complete the story of Morgan. After the burial of Lot the tale of Balain is taken up in earnest with a reference to the dolorous stroke and the battle of Salisbury Plain, the stroke to come at the end of *The Tale of Balain* many hundreds of lines later, and the battle to take place in the *Death of Arthur* hundreds of pages later.

Now the diagram would look like this: R - L - B - R - L - B.

Not only have the threads of Rion and Lot's adventures been woven together, but the adventures of Balain have been gradually introduced over a space of many hundreds of pages to prepare the reader for the climactic dolorous stroke and the resulting destruction and torment which will last twenty-two years and culminate in the death of Arthur, the destruction of the realm, the flower of chivalry, and the return of Escalibor to the lake whence it came. This elaborate structure may be too complex to be immediately grasped by the modern reader. What at first seems to be an endless series of disjointed episodes, finally emerges as a powerfully made whole, if one has the memory to apprehend it. One almost has to sit down with a pencil and make lists in order to hold it all in mind. Unaccustomed as we are to this sort of arrangement, we run the very real risk of missing it altogether.

Given such a structure, one is then tempted to ask: what purpose does it serve? One possible answer is that the incredible complexity of the cycle with its beautifully interwoven fabric has a strangely compelling force for the reader who is attuned to the "frequency" of the work. For example, the abrupt juxtaposition of unrelated events in this prose narrative has the same sort of effect that one might find in T. S. Eliot's poetry. As Genesius Jones put it in his brilliant book on Eliot, *Approach to the Purpose*:

> His act is an intuitive recognition of a parallel and his juxtaposition of the two attitudes is an attempt to discover by interplay new meaning: to establish the possibility of deeper penetration into the transcendental insight than is given by either of the intuitions alone.[7]

7. (London: Hodder & Stoughton, 1964), p. 27.

What Mr. Jones is explaining here with reference to Eliot's reaction to French symbolist poetry of the nineteenth century, in order to elucidate Eliot's use of words, might well apply to *The Romance of the Grail*. When in a piece of prose or verse the author juxtaposes words, symbols, events, feelings, or sensations, whether they have a direct *causal* relationship with their neighbors or not, each remains individual, but its proximity to its neighbors on the page, then in the memory of the reader, brings forth a new whole which is different from any of its parts. Such is the "logic of the imagination" as it was understood by Eliot and as it was known to the author of the thirteenth-century cyclic romance.[8]

The second striking effect of the structure of the Balain story in its larger context could be called "dramatic distance."[9] The development of the tale of the conflict between Arthur and Rion occupies sixty-two pages off and on, and the interesting thing about it is that it is not continuous.[10] It is incessantly interrupted by totally unrelated matters. If those intervening passages or interlace elements were removed the remaining material would form a continuous narrative.

8. The term "logic of the imagination" was used by Eliot and taken up by Jones; it describes the habit of mind represented by Eliot's poetry and by medieval romance admirably well. For the professional philosopher's view, see Henry B. Veatch, *Two Logics: The Conflict between Classical and Neo-Analytic Philosophy* (Evanston, Ill.: Northwestern University Press, 1969).

9. The term "dramatic distance" is one that I have coined. See my article on the *Méraugis de Portlesguez*: "Form and Meaning in the *Méraugis de Portlesguez* by Raoul de Houdenc," *Genre*, II, no. 1, (1969), 9–20.

10. On the nature of interlace as a structural device, there is a rather large and growing bibliography. Perhaps the best single work on the subject is Eugène Vinaver, *The Rise of Romance* (New York: Oxford University Press, 1971), espec. pp. x, 158.

The effect of this device is that each time the story is interrupted only to be continued many lines later, the reader is forced to make an effort to recall the circumstances that have been presented before as a background to what he is reading now. The effect of these gaps is to force a conscious effort which renews the impact of a former event while etching the present segment of the story more deeply into the mind. The dramatic effect is enhanced more than it could be if each sub-tale were developed one at a time, straight through from beginning to end. Instead of the usual curve to represent dramatic development,

this technique might be represented graphically like this:

The pauses increase the effect by forcing the reader to put off the pleasure of further development and *dénouement,* just as a child sometimes heightens his pleasure of eating a piece of cake by putting off the frosting until last, in order to add to his experience the pleasure of anticipation. Each sub-tale—and there are innumerable ones similarly woven into the fabric—acts like one thread in a tapestry: hence the term "interlace." They hold each other together and, by their close juxtaposition and interrupted continuity, form a dazzling literary fabric. What Ferdinand Lot wrote in 1918 in his *Etude sur le Lancelot en prose* could be said about *The Romance of the Grail:*

> ...le Lancelot n'est pas une mosaïque d'où l'on pourrait avec adresse enlever des cubes pour les remplacer par d'autres, c'est une

sparterie ou une tapisserie : si l'on tente d'y pratiquer une coupure, tout part en morceaux.[11]

Lot's remark went unnoticed until the publication of Eugène Vinaver's first edition of the works of Sir Thomas Malory in 1947. In this edition appeared the first statement of the fact that interlace was an aesthetic phenomenon which was the structural framework of the medieval French cyclic romance. Brief mention of the phenomenon had been made by C. S. Lewis in 1936 in his *Allegory of Love* and again in 1952 in his introduction to the Spenser selection in *Major British Authors*.

Then, in 1966, in his Presidential Address to the Modern Humanities Research Association, Professor Vinaver showed that the interlace phenomenon is present not only in literary structure but also in the graphic art of the period, which may suggest that the phenomenon is representative of an aesthetic "habit of mind" of that period.

Since that time several scholars such as John Leyerle, Wilhelm Kellermann, Richard Terdiman, Jean Gaudon, Robert Jordan, and myself have studied interlace and related phenomena in various works of literary and graphic art.[12] An example of such a piece can be seen in the frontispiece of

11. Ferdinand Lot, *Etude sur le Lancelot en prose* (Paris: Champion, 1918), pp. 17 ff.

12. John Leyerle, "The Interlace Structure of *Beowulf*," *University of Toronto Quarterly*, XXXVII, no. 1 (October 1967), 1–17; Wilhelm Kellerman, "Aufbaustil und Weltbild Chrestiens von Troyes im Percevalroman," Beiheft 88 zur *ZfRP* (Halle, 1936), p. 35; Richard Terdiman, "The Structure of Villon's *Testament*," *PMLA*, XXCII, pt. 2, 622–633; Jean Gaudon, "Eloge de la digression," *Travaux de linguistique et de littérature publiés par le Centre de Philologie et de littératures romanes de l'Université de Strasbourg* (Strasbourg, 1968), pp. 125–47; Robert M. Jordan, *Chaucer and the Shape of Creation* (Cambridge, Mass.: Harvard University Press, 1967), pp. xviii, 257; David E. Campbell, *Méraugis de Portlesguez*.

this book. Since interlace is the organizing principle of the larger work of which *The Tale of Balain* forms a part, restoring the passage omitted by Miss Legge is of capital importance if the reader is to apprehend the work as it was originally conceived.

Now that we have seen how the Balain episode fits into *The Romance of the Grail,* let us examine its internal structure. This tale is the culmination of a long process of composition that might be called *elaborative accretion.* This process corresponds to a mode of thought which has wide cultural implications. In discussing the laïcization of French and English societies in the thirteenth century, J. R. Strayer, in his recent book *Medieval Statecraft and the Perspectives of History,* explains the background against which the cyclic romances were composed:

> The thirteenth century was a legalistic century, a century in which men sought exact definitions of all human relationships, a century in which men wanted to *work out the logical implications of all general ideas* and projects, a century in which men wanted *to complete and justify the work of their predecessors.* And because the thirteenth century was legalistic, because it was a period of definitions and detailed explanations, it was a much less tolerant century than the twelfth. It was no longer possible to harmonize divergent views by thinking of them as merely different aspects of universal truth [italics added].[13]

When the author who fashioned *The Romance of the Grail* set out to rework the materials he had at hand, he was faced with a task of incredible complexity. The principal difficulty was that the material he had to work with was not elaborate enough to suit him, though each part was quite lucid in its

13. (Princeton, N. J.: Princeton University Press, 1971).

own right. He felt he must "elucidate" the previously exist-ingmaterialandleave open the possibility ofany future devel-opments he or a successor might wish to set forth, since, as Professor Strayer has pointed out, the thirteenth was a century in which men wanted "to complete and justify the work of their predecessors." Our author felt he had to adopt a method of composition which would be spacious enough to accommodate expansion. The framework he was bound to choose was structural interlace, which permitted him to use artificial order freely. Interlace was an integral part of the aesthetic environment of the day and was the only structure he could turn to, to solve the dilemma posed by his materials.

The effect of this method of expansion in reverse is ap-parent in the relationship between *The Tale of Balain* and the *Vulgate Quest of the Holy Grail,* which was composed ten years earlier. At the beginning of the *Quest,* Arthur and his company have sat down to eat when suddenly all the doors and windows of the hall bang shut by themselves and the room is lit by a strange light. As they wonder at this marvel, an old man dressed in a white robe comes in, leading by the hand a knight dressed in red who has no sword or shield. The old man says:

> Peace be with you. King Arthur, I bring to you the Desired Knight, the one who descends from the high lineage of King David and who is related to Joseph of Arimathea, the one through whom the enchantments on this and foreign lands will be ended. See him here.[14]

14. *La Queste del Saint Graal,* ed. Albert Pauphilet, Classiques Français du Moyen Age, Vol. 33 (Paris: Champion, 1967), p. 7, ll. 25–28: "Rois Artus, je t'ameign le Chevalier Desirré, celui qui est estraiz dou haut lignage le Roi David et del parenté Joseph d'Arimacie celui par cui les merveilles de cest païs et des estranges terres remaindront. Veez le ci."

And Arthur responds:

> Sir, welcome if these words are true and welcome to the knight
> as well! For if he is the one we are waiting for to accomplish the
> adventures of the Holy Grail, never has a man been feted as well
> as we will him.[15]

The *Quest* then goes on to tell of Galahad's wanderings:
how he puts an end to one after the other of the magical
phenomena current in the kingdom, and how finally he sees
the mysteries of the Grail, is transfigured, and ascends to
Heaven. Nowhere in the text, however, is any explanation
offered of what caused these magical phenomena, or why
such a holy person as Galahad is needed to undo them, or
what purpose all that serves. Nor is there any explanation
offered in the sections of the *Vulgate* which precede the
Quest, although there are some premonitions of what is to
come.

These questions go unanswered in the *Vulgate*. Then, ten
years later, when our author set out to compile *The Romance
of the Grail,* he undertook to answer them. It is *The Tale of
Balain* which contains the answers: the marvels were ini-
tiated by Balain's dolorous stroke; Balain's accursed fate
could only be counterbalanced by Galahad, the pure and
perfect knight; it is because of Balain's *mescheance* and the
events surrounding his misadventures that all these forces
are set in motion which will eventually lead to the destruction of Logres, of Arthurian chivalry, and of Arthur himself.

This is how expansion in reverse works: the author of *The
Romance of the Grail* sets out to explain the events written of

---

15. *Ibid.,* ll. 30–33: "Sire, bien soiez vos venuz se ceste parole est veraie, et
bien soit li chevaliers venus! Car se ce est cil que nos atendions a achever les
aventures del Saint Graal, onques si grant joie ne fut fete d'ome come nos ferons
de lui."

in the earlier *Vulgate* by expanding his narrative to include what he imagined to have been their background. He adds the expanded passage in the proper place in his own tale, before his own version of the *Quest*. The development of a work in this way from one writer to the next throughout time is composition by elaborative accretion on the level of an entire cycle: the corpus gains in volume while the use of materials becomes more and more elaborate.

The development of the Waste Land theme, then, from its early form to the form it finally takes in the Balain story, is an example of the process of elaborative accretion on the level of an element of a cycle.[16] The story consists of four themes: the miraculous weapon, the wounded king or knight and the blow that wounded him, the dolorous stroke, the land laid waste, and the healing of the wound. These elements occur separately and in groups of two and three in texts from about 1180 onward, but are not finally linked together until about 1230 or 1235 with the composition of *The Romance of the Grail* of which the present text forms a part.[17] In a late version of *The Quest of the Holy Grail* the maimed king says to Galahad, who is about to heal his wound: "Look at the dolorous stroke which the Knight with the Two Swords struck. Because of this stroke many evil things have happened. It grieves me." [18]

This is the end product of the process of elaborative accretion. Here the four elements are brought together in one structure. The process is complete. Thus *The Tale of Balain*

---

16. For a detailed development of this problem, see *The Rise of Romance*, chap. IV, "The Waste Land," pp. 53–67. .

17. Cf. Bogdanow, *The Romance of the Grail*, passim.

18. This statement is found in MS. BN. fr. 343, fol. 103ª. "Veez ci li doloreux cop que li chevaliers as Deux Espees fist. Par cestui cop sunt maint mal avenu. Ce me poise."

has two identities: it is an element of a larger whole, the cyclic romance of the Grail, and it is the result of a long process of composition spanning many years and involving many authors or *remanieurs*. As Professor Vinaver writes:

> ...what we have before us is not an organic pattern originally conceived as a whole, but a product of an ingenious "assembling" of the existing elements in a new sequence.[19]

All of the elements that have been assembled in some of the ways explained above were not new to the author of *The Romance of the Grail*, nor are they new to us. However, they are presented in this translation as they were in the thirteenth century, not as they have been rearranged and "modernized" by more recent artists. In this text the reader will find much that is unfamiliar to him: the characters are "flat," the adventures are sometimes improbable and often fantastic, the motivations are obscure, and the language may appear childish. But one should not be stopped by what is merely unfamiliar. It is in the slow savoring of the unfolding convolutions of the structure that the reader will find his pleasure in reading the story of the accursed knight. If he perseveres he will glimpse the secrets of form that have caused this medieval tale to last so long and be loved by so many.

Perhaps a word about the techniques of translation would be appropriate here. I have attempted to follow the French text as closely as possible without doing violence to English syntax and vocabulary. I have also tried to render the narrative in a natural way that will pose no barrier of understanding to the reader of modern English. I have modernized spellings and vocabulary so that the language will not seem artificially archaic or stilted, but at the same time I have

19. *The Rise of Romance*, p. 65.

taken care not to stray too far from the literal meaning of the text. To walk the fine line between contemporary usage and the literal translation is, of course, quite difficult. But the essential point here is to make this medieval text accessible to the contemporary reader in a way which is as natural to him as possible, while not betraying its meaning. Notes in the present volume have been held to a minimum.

I would like to take this opportunity to express my grateful appreciation to the students of my Introductory Studies classes at Northwestern University, whose enthusiastic response to medieval literature has encouraged me to do this work. My debt to Professor Eugène Vinaver is vast. Contact with his learned and subtle mind has stimulated my own efforts, and his loyal friendship has encouraged me to persevere in the study of medieval literature and in the dissemination of the fruits of that study.

Thanks are also due to the Committee for Medieval Studies, particularly its chairman, Norman B. Spector, who has supported my efforts, as well as to my excellent typist, Miss Holly Krohn, and to the Northwestern University Press for its indulgence in seeing the book into print.

The Tale of Balain

ONE DAY THE KING WAS SEATED AT HIS DINNER and had already finished his meal. It happened that while they all were chatting in the palace they saw a knight enter the hall. He was on horseback and fully armed, but he was in such condition that the blood ran out of his side in more than three places and his horse was in such a state from running fast that it fell down under him in the midst of the palace as soon as he entered. The knight, who was quite swift and agile, jumped down and said to the king,

"Sire, I am bringing you news which is most troublesome and bad. King Rion has invaded your land with a host greater than any you have ever seen. He is burning and laying waste your land and killing your men wherever he finds them, and I don't know how many of your castles he has already taken. If you don't take some action you will soon have lost your whole domain."

The king, who listened to this news, answered the knight,

"Where did you last see King Rion? Take care that you tell me the truth."

"Sire, I left him at one of your castles that they call Terrabel, where he had besieged the castle with such a great host that it was indeed a marvel."

"Let him lay siege," said the king. "I shall have it lifted quite soon, much to his shame, if God please."

Then he commanded his people to disarm the knight and to conduct him to chambers and take care of him. They did as they were told. The king commanded that they speedily make up dispatches and send them this way and that to his barons to tell them to come without delay and with all haste to Camelot. When the barons heard that the king requested their presence in time of such need, they equipped themselves as quickly as they could and hurried to the city. Thus you could have seen assembled within three months more than four thousand knights, of whom even the most cowardly felt brave and hardy. Thus the king had summoned his men and they came, a formidable host.

The day that he was supposed to start out for battle there came a damsel, rich and greatly beauteous. And it was one of the damsels of the lady known as the Lady of Avalon and she said to the king,

"To you, o king, my Lady of the Isle of Avalon sends me so that I might be helped and succoured in your court in a matter which grieves me much and of which I think I will never be delivered if I am not saved from it in your court."

Then she took off her neck the mantle which she was wearing and said to the king,

"O king, here is the sword which I have put on as you can see, but know that I cannot do with it what I wish; neither extract it from the scabbard nor take it off, for this is not a thing which is allowed of any woman or any knight unless he be the best knight in the land and the most loyal: a knight without treachery, guileless, and innocent of treason. Whoever is such will be able to untie the thong of the sword and take it with him and deliver me from a thing which is annoying me greatly. For as long as I have the sword with me every day, I will never be able to have either rest or peace."

When the king heard what the damsel said, he answered,

"Young lady, you amaze me greatly. For it seems to me that anybody could indeed take off that sword that you have tied around you."

"Let it be known, sire, that it is not like you think, for no one can take it off if he is not the way I've described him to be."

"By my faith," said the king, "let each one try, those who are knights, for it will be a great honor to him who is able to untie it. If he accomplishes this, he will show that he is the best knight in his country and that he is the best endowed, as you have said. Since I am the lord of this land and of all those who are here, I will attempt first, not because I think I am the best knight in the country but to give the example to the others."

Then King Arthur rose from where he was seated and came to the damsel and took hold of the cords of the sword and thought he could untie them, because he imagined that these were straps like on other swords, but he could not. The lady said to him,

"Aha, king, you need not apply such great strength, for force

4

will not succeed. He who accomplishes this adventure will in no wise exert such great effort."

Then the king went to sit down and said to those who were with him,

"This deed is not for me to do. So now all of you try and whomever God favors, let him accomplish it."

And then all the barons and lords attempted, one after the other, but none was able to untie the straps. Thus all those who were there tried except a poor knight who was born in Northumberland. He had been disinherited by the King of Northumberland because he had killed a relative of the king's, he had been put in prison for more than six months, had just come out, and was so poor that he hardly had a thing at all. Although he was poor in possessions he was rich in heart, courage, and prowess and in all the realm of Logres there was not a better knight than he. Since he seemed so poor no one made any mention of him, because scarcely anyone who is poor is treated well among the rich. All those in the palace, poor and rich, had tried the sword except this one. The king, who thought everyone had come, said to the damsel,

"Lady, you're going to have to go somewhere else if you want to be free, for it seems to me you will find no one here who can deliver you. This grieves me sorely, for if someone in my household could have accomplished this thing I would have derived great honor from it."

"Ah, great God," said she, "so must I, disappointed, leave this court where there are so many good men and good knights? Certainly I do not know where I shall go if I have failed here, for I have already been in the court of King Rion, where I could find no more help than I did here now."

"Lady," said the king, "we cannot give you more help now, since it does not please our Lord."

"Ah, God," she cried, "it seems to me that now I will be condemned to bear this burden, this martyrdom, and this pain forever, and I have not deserved it."

Then the damsel began to cry copiously and said that she would leave, commending the king and all his company to God. When the poor knight saw that she would not remain longer, that she was leaving right away, he jumped forward in front of the other knights. He was very sad that no one had asked him to try the sword as the others had done. So he hailed the damsel and said to her, within hearing of all the others,

"Ah, young lady, if you please, wait until I have tried the sword as the others have done."

When she saw that he appeared to be so poor, she couldn't help saying to him,

"Certainly, sir knight, I think that you will try it for naught, for I could not believe it to be true that you are the best knight in this hall where there are assembled so many good ones."

And he was all ashamed and answered angrily,

"Young lady, don't hold me in scorn for my poverty. I was once much wealthier. Moreover, there is no one here whom I would refuse to meet in battle."

Then he took the straps of the sword and put his hands on the knots and untied them easily and took the sword in his hand. Then he said to the maiden,

"Now you can go free when you wish, but the sword will stay with me because I believe that I have earned it."

And he drew it from the scabbard and began to look at it and saw that it was beautiful and goodly in appearance. Never had he seen any other that he prized as much. Then he put it back in the scabbard, and the damsel said to him straight out,

"Sir knight, you have delivered me and in this you have won great honor, for it is proven and quite apparent by this deed that you are the best knight here. Nonetheless, even though you have saved me it was no part of your covenant that the sword would become yours, and I beg of you that you give it back to me, since you must be as courteous as you are valiant."

The knight said that he would not give her the sword back, even if he were thought to be a villain by all those in the court.

"I say to you," said she, "that if you take it away with you misfortune will befall you. For know this well, that the man that you kill first with it will be the man whom you love most in the world."

And he said that he would take away the sword, even if he himself were to be killed by it.

"Very well," said she, "so be it because you want it that way. And know well this, that you will not have it more than two months before you will regret it. But I will tell you another marvel. Know that it will come to pass as I'm about to tell you. Before this year has passed you will fight a knight who will kill you with a sword and you will kill him. And because I didn't want this misfortune to happen to a good knight such as you, I wanted to carry it away. With God as my witness, as long as no knight carried it, you wouldn't have to worry about dying by arms. Now carry it away with you if it pleases you, and know well that you carry your death with you."

The sword seemed so good and beautiful to him that even if death must come of it he would take it just the same. He said to one of his squires who was standing by him,

"Go! Bring my arms and bring my horse, for I will no longer remain at this court because they have shown me very clearly at this place that poverty causes many a good man to be treated ill."

The squire left to execute the orders of his lord, and the king saw this thing and was quite ashamed of what he heard the knight say. He came to him and said,

"Ah, sir knight, for the sake of God, don't be grieved that I have been discourteous toward you. I am prepared to make it up to you in any way you wish and according to your desires, but truly I did not know you so I must not be blamed. There are so many good men here that I didn't know which one to choose. Stay here now, sir knight, I beg you. And I'll promise you that as long as I shall live I will never fail to be your companion, for there is nothing now that you could ask of me that I would not give to you, if I could, provided that you stay in my house."

7

The knight answered that he would not stay this time, no matter how much anyone begged him to nor for any gift that they might give him.

The king said that this thing was very sad because he had not seen for a long time any knight in his court whose company he wished to have as much as the company of this one.

All those who were present talked a great deal of the knight who brought to its conclusion the adventure in which all the others had failed. Some of them said that he knew about enchantments, and that he did it through them rather than through his own valor. While they were in the midst of discussing these things, in came a damsel on horseback and while still mounted she came up to the king and said to him,

"King, you owe me a boon. Acquit yourself of your debt before these gentlemen here assembled."

The king looked at the maiden and recognized that she was the one who had given him the sword and answered,

"Certainly, maiden, I do owe you a gift and I will do my duty by you to the best of my ability. But if it please you, tell me one thing which I forgot to ask you."

"And what is it?" said she.

"It is the name of the sword that you gave me."[1]

"Let it be known," said she, "that the sword is called by its correct name of Excalibur."

"Now ask," said he, "whatever pleases you, for I will give it to you if I can."

"I ask you," said she, "for the head of the young lady who brought this sword here or that of the knight who has it. And do you know," she said, "why I ask such an unusual gift? Be in-

1. Since the name she gives in answer is Excalibur, this might be the Lady of the Lake who gave Arthur the sword. Since she always sponsored good works and was the protector of Lancelot in the earlier *Vulgate Lancelot Proper*, it is unlikely that she would have been responsible for the death of Balain's brother (not Balaan, but another brother), but as is often the case in Arthurian romance, the dilemma is left unresolved by the text.

formed that this knight killed one of my brothers, a worthy man and a good knight, and that this young lady caused my father to be killed. For this reason I would truly like to be avenged upon one or the other."

When the king heard this request, he recoiled, astonished, and said,

"Damsel, in the name of God, I beg you that you ask me something else. For it is certain that in granting you this boon I would be doing my duty toward you in a very wrong way, for there is no one who could not accuse me of an evil and treacherous action if I had either one of these two killed who have done me no harm."

When the knight heard what the damsel asked the lord, he came to her and said,

"Ah, damsel, I've been looking for you for a long time. It's been more than three years that I've been searching for you. You were the one who destroyed my brother with poison. Because I hated you so mortally and because I couldn't find you, I killed your brother. But since it so happens that I found you here, I shall never search for you anywhere else."

Then he drew the sword from the scabbard. When the damsel saw him coming at her, she started for the door of the hall to escape from his hands. Then he said to her,

"I do you this same service. Rather than let you ask the king for my head, I will give him yours."

Then he made a leap toward the young lady and struck with the sword so forcefully that he caused her head to fly to the ground. Then he took the sword and the head and came to the king and said,

"Sire, now know you that you see here the head of the most treacherous damsel who ever entered your court. Great misfortune would befall you if she had remained for a long time in your court and many evil things would have happened to you. I'm telling you that it is certain that no greater joy has filled any land than will spread across the land of Northumberland as soon as they know she is dead."

When the king saw this deed, he was very angry and answered the knight,

"Certainly, noble knight, you have committed the greatest treachery I have ever seen committed by a knight such as I thought you were. I did not think that any knight, be he foreigner or of my privy council, would have been so foolhardy as to cause me as great a shame as you have. For what greater shame could anyone have caused me than by killing before me a damsel who was under my safe conduct and whom I had to protect. For since she was in my hall she should have had no cause to fear anyone or anything that might have harmed her, but my house should have guaranteed her safety against anyone as long as she was within its walls. Such were the manner and the custom of my castle which you have violated and destroyed mainly through your pride. And I am telling you that even if you were my brother you would repent of this deed. Now leave my court quickly and go forth, and know this, I will never be content until such great pride has been avenged."

When the knight heard that the king was so angry about this thing, he saw that he had erred greatly and committed a great crime in killing the damsel in front of the king himself. Then he knelt in front of the king and said,

"Ah, sire, have mercy upon me, for God's sake. I recognize indeed that I have committed a grave fault. For the sake of God, pardon me, if it pleases you."

The king said that he had no desire to pardon him.

"No, sire? Now at least have enough courtly grace, since I came to your court, that I might have a truce with you and your men."

"Indeed," said the king, "you will not have it, and I beg them and require that they do everything to avenge this shame, for they also suffer from it as do I. Since, neither for my sake nor for theirs did you abandon your plan, we can truly say that you had little regard for us, you who did not forego your crime for fear of us nor for the sake of our honor. Now leave here, for you will find nothing else in my heart at this time."

As soon as the knight had understood that he could get no further nor be pardoned for his crime, he rose from in front of the king, left the court, and went to his lodging. All this time he was carrying the maiden's head with him. When he arrived at his lodging, he sought out his squire and said to him,

"You see here the head of the damsel for whom I have been searching so long."

"And where did you find it?" said the squire.

And he told him straightaway how she had come before the king and how she had asked for his head, and he told him further-more everything that happened, the king's answer, and about his departure from the court.

Then the youth began to weep bitterly and said to his lord,

"Oh, my lord, you've done a bad thing if by your crime you've lost the good will of the king and of the court because of this damsel. What a calamity that she was ever born!"

"Now don't be dismayed," said he, "for if by my crime I have lost the good will of the king, I shall, very soon, if God please, do such that he will be appeased toward me, if any honest knight can be appeased by the prowess a man may have."

"What do you want to do?" said the squire.

"I want," said the knight, "to bring him the head of his most mortal enemy, of him whom he fears the most just now, or send him alive to his prison."

"And who is he?" said the squire.

"He is," said he, "King Rion, the most powerful man in the world nowadays, excepting only King Arthur. But however powerful he may be, I hope, with the help of God, to put him at King Arthur's mercy. And this would be a thing through which I would make my peace with King Arthur if ever I could."

"May God grant you the power to do it," said the youth, "for certainly I hope very much that it will happen as you have said."

"I shall tell you in truth," said the knight, "what you shall do. You shall leave me and go to the kingdom of Northumberland and carry with you the head of the damsel. You will show it to my friends wherever you find them. Then you can tell them that I have avenged myself upon her who killed my brother, in a place where there were many of the best knights in the world."

He said that he would indeed carry out the errand but he asked where he could find him when he came back.

"I think," he said, "that you will find me at King Arthur's court. For before you get back, if God please, I will have made my peace with the king."

Then he took his armor, mounted his horse, put on the sword he got from the damsel beside the one he had carried before, so that he had two at his side.[2] He took a shield and a heavy and strong lance and left the city and headed for the place where he thought King Rion was with all his host. The squire left in the other direction and commended his lord to God, and the knight went thus with the two swords.

And because of the two swords that he carried, as long as he lived thereafter, he lost his original name, for they used to call him Balain the Wild, and a brother of his who was no less of a knight than he they called Balaan the Wild. And this Balain later begat Dodinel the Wild, who subsequently was a companion of the Round Table and was renowned for his great deeds and prowess. But Balain later lost his name because of the two swords he carried so that he was no longer called Balain, but they all called him the Knight with the Two Swords. And he was everywhere known by this name. If he had lived longer, he would have been more famous than anyone who carried arms in the realm of Logres. But it did not please Our Lord that he last long, and he himself was somewhat to blame, for he undertook to accomplish such great things in order to make his peace with the king; there was no adventure far or near that he heard tell of that he didn't embark upon. He did so much in that first year that he will be talked about

2. Here he is referring to his own sword and the sword with the enchanted belt ("The Sword with the Strange Hangings," which appears in many Arthurian romances), which he took from the first maiden against her will (cf. p. 7).

forever. Because he didn't refuse to meet in battle anyone he met, he died when he met his brother, with whom he fought, and they both died together, having failed to recognize each other, and this was a grievous loss. For they were both such good knights that in the whole realm of Logres there weren't two warriors as good.

But now the tale leaves off speaking of them and returns to King Arthur.

Now the tale tells that when the knight had left the palace carrying both swords, the king fell into deep thought, for the insult the knight had done in his very court grieved him sorely. He asked those that were in his court,

"What can one do with this knight who has thus broken the custom of my court and my household? I did not think that anybody could be so brazen as to dare commit such a great outrage in front of me and in front of so many good knights as are now here. Now give me advice, for I don't want anyone, no matter how highly-placed or good a man he be, to become accustomed to committing toward me so great a folly as this one has done."

Then came foreward an Irish knight who was thought to be most valiant, and he thought that he was without doubt one of the best of knights and so he certainly was. And although he was not as good a knight as he thought, he was quite envious of the one who had achieved the adventure of the sword in which he had failed. And he thought it had been done through fraud of some kind, because he couldn't believe that any knight had more prowess in him than he had. He said to the king,

"Sire, if it pleases you, I will avenge you and this court for the great shame that he has done in such a way that I will make known to the knight the outrage that he has committed, if only I thought that you wouldn't hold it against me."

"Never," said the king, "would I hold it against you or anyone here, but on the contrary, I indeed call upon you to do whatever would enhance the honor of the court. For I don't want others to adopt such customs."

The knight thanked him very much for this and departed and

came to his lodgings, asked for his arms, and had his horse saddled. And when he was armed as best he could, he mounted his horse, took his shield and sword, and went off at great speed on the traces of Balain. But now the tale leaves off speaking of him and goes back to King Arthur and the damsel who had brought the sword.

The tale tells that after the Irish knight had left the court in pursuit of Balain, the king had the body of the slain damsel carried into a room in the castle to perform all the rites which all Christian people did in those days. But the tale now falls silent about him and says that at this point Merlin came in and when he saw the damsel who brought the sword, he said to her,

"Why did you come here? Cursed be he who sent you here, and you for coming, for your arrival has done nothing but damage to the court."

Then he turned to the king and said to him,

"King Arthur, now know you truly that this damsel is the most treacherous who has ever come to your court, and I will show you how. It is true that she has a brother, a very good knight, brave and courageous, much younger than she. This maiden, as I well know, loved a knight who is the most disloyal and dishonest in the realm of Logres. So it happened that the knight who was this maiden's brother, encountered, by chance, the one she loved. They charged each other and fought so fiercely that the brother slew the lady's friend. She was so despondent over this that she said she would never rest easy until she had arranged the death of her brother. She was very close with the Lady of the Isle of Avalon. She begged her at such length that she be avenged upon her brother who had slain her lover that the lady said she would help her. She then girded her with the sword that she brought to this court and said to her,

'It must be that he who unties this sword is the best knight in the land and the truest and the purest. Search for him until you find him. Know that he who will free you from this sword will put your brother to death by dint of knightly prowess and thus will avenge you upon him with whom you are so mortally angry.' Thus the treacherous girl took the sword so that her brother would face death and so he will, because he will soon be killed by it. Now see what great misfortune will come at her instigation. It seems to me, truly, that she would have deserved to die more than she who died here a while ago."

"In the name of God, Merlin," said the king, "you speak the truth. Indeed it seems to me that killing her was unjust."

And when the maid understood that the king agreed with Merlin, she remained no longer in the court, so she left in haste. The king said to Merlin,

"Merlin, what can be done about the knight who despised so much my court and all those in it that he did not hesitate to kill the damsel in front of us all?"

"Ah! sire," said Merlin, "don't speak more of her death. It is indeed a shame that he is not to survive long, for he is a marvelous man and a good knight. Know that during this decade no knight will die in your court whose death you will regret as much as this one when you learn that he has died. For this reason I beg of you, sire, for God's sake, to pardon him for his crime, for be advised that to such a man one should pardon a grave misdeed. And certainly, if you knew him as well as I know him, you would be sorry for what you said to him. As for you, my lords, who blame him for this evil deed, I beg you to hold ill will toward him no longer. For know well that he will fully amend his fault at court before long. He will demonstrate that he deserves to have the sword more than any man now living."

"Ah! Merlin," said the king, "it seems to me that you know him well. For God's sake, tell me who he is."

"I tell you," said Merlin, "that his name is Balain the Wild, and he is, I know it for sure, the best knight in the world, for which I feel sorry for him. For he will meet his death in the realm of Logres before his time."

When the barons heard what Merlin said, they restrained themselves from the hostile feelings they harbored toward the knight, and each one prayed for him and asked that Our Lord guide him wherever he might go. The king himself was no longer as angry as he had been, for he believed Merlin in whatever he said, and he wished then that he had not spoken to the knight so harshly.

"O king," said Merlin, "you have recognized his merit too late. Know that he will never again pay homage to you nor be of your company for any length of time. It is a shame."

Thus they all talked about the knight. And the king said to Merlin,

"What do you have to tell me about King Rion? Will he be able to harm me in any way?"

"Go on your way, my King," said Merlin, "in the assurance that Our Lord will do you a greater honor than you think. He has not put you in the place of great glory you're in to let you stumble so soon. Thus, do not be dismayed, for he will help you wherever you are, if you do not default."

Thus Merlin spoke to the king and admonished him about the knight. The king answered that he was sore aggrieved about the things he had said to him. But here the tale says no more of them and goes back to the knight from Ireland as he left his lodgings.

So says the tale that when the knight had left his lodgings, armed as he was, he rode out of the city and found the tracks of the knight who had preceded him. Although he did not know him very well, chance led him in the same path that the other had taken. He galloped in such a manner and at such a speed that at the foot of a mountain he overtook the knight he was seeking. He shouted at him from afar as soon as he thought he could hear,

"Sir knight, turn that shield this way, or I'll strike you from behind, and you will be all the more shamed."

At these words he looked at Balain and realized that he would have to joust with him on the spot. Balain said to him loud enough so that he could hear,

"Knight, before you joust with me tell me who is your lord."

And he replied,

"My lord is King Arthur who sent me here for your destruction. I challenge you so beware of me, for you must joust."

And Balain answered,

16

"I am truly grieved that he is your lord. For if I kill you, then I will be more guilty in his eyes than I was before, and in this way I will pile evil deed upon evil deed."

Then Balain wheeled his horse toward him, drew his shield up against his chest, and lowered his lance. The Irish knight charged against him at as great a speed as the horse could muster and pierced his shield and broke his lance in the midst of his chest, but did not budge him out of the saddle. Balain struck him so hard that he pierced his shield, broke the links of his mail, and planted his lance in his body so that the steel and a large part of the shaft appeared on the other side. He hit with great force, so that he bore him to the ground over the flanks of the horse. And when he withdrew the lance, the man, who felt death coming on, fell quiet. Balain went to the end of his charge, turned, and drew his sword, because he didn't think the knight was dead yet. When he came up to him and stood there a moment he saw that the ground all around him was red with his blood. Then he saw that he was indeed dead and he was aggrieved because the knight was of the house of King Arthur. He began to think about what he could do, for he would willingly have paid him some honor if he could have.

And while he was meditating in this way, a maiden came along as fast as her horse could carry her. When she came near the place where the knight lay, she dismounted rapidly, because she didn't think he was dead yet. When she saw him and recognized him, she made such a great dole that anyone watching her would have said that he had never seen such a thing. She fainted again and again. When she recovered from her fainting spell and could speak, she said to Balain,

"Alas, my lord, you have killed two hearts in one, and two bodies in one and you have lost two souls for one."

Then she took the knight's sword, withdrew it from the scabbard, and said,

"My love, I must follow you, for I think I have too long avoided Death. If He is as kind as He seems, no one will die as easily as we."

Then she struck herself so hard in the chest with the sword that it pierced her heart. She was near the dead knight, and Balain, who saw that she intended to kill herself, wanted to snatch the sword out of her hands, but was not quick enough to do it before she struck herself.

When he saw this happen he didn't know what to say, for he was so astonished that he didn't know whether he was asleep or awake. He had never seen in this world a thing which amazed him as much as this one did. He said to himself that the maiden loved truly and that he hadn't thought such true love could enter into the heart of woman.

While he was observing this thing, trying to decide what he could do with both of them, because he didn't want to abandon them, he looked toward the forest and saw Balaan, his brother, come out of it, fully armed, and accompanied by only one squire. When Balain saw him coming he went to meet him and shouted that he was glad to see him. When the other heard him, he knew him by his arms, which he had seen once before. As soon as he recognized him he threw his helmet off his head and ran to embrace him and then cried out of joy and emotion. And he said,

"Oh, brother, I thought I'd never see you again! By what stroke of luck were you delivered from the miserable prison where you were?"

Balain answered that the king's daughter herself set him free and if it hadn't been for her he'd still be there.

"But what chance brought you this way?"

"In truth," said Balaan, "they told me at the Castle of the Four Stones that you had been freed and that you had been seen at King Arthur's court. And so I was going there in great haste, thinking I would find you. So tell me whether you've been there."

Balain said he'd just come from there.

"And why did you leave?"

So he told him then everything he had seen, about the court and the sword and the maiden he had killed, the reason for his leaving the court so soon (for otherwise he would have stayed longer in the company of the other knights); and how even since he left he had been unlucky enough to kill this knight. It aggrieved him sorely.

"And this maiden," said Balaan, "how did she die?"

And Balain told him straightaway. Then Balaan told him that the maiden loved truly, and because of the devotion that was in her he will never fail to come to the aid of a lady whenever she would require it.

"And what, brother Balaan, can we do with these bodies?"

He said that he could give no advice in the matter, God help him.

While they were discussing these things, along came a dwarf who had come out of the city and came as fast as the horse could carry him. When he came upon the bodies and recognized them, he began to moan and groan and pull his hair and clap his hands. When he had carried on in this way for some time, he asked the two knights,

"Tell me which of you killed this man."

And Balain answered,

"Why do you ask?"

"Because," said he, "I want to know."

"I say that I killed him, but it was in self defense, and it didn't please me, God help me, so it grieved me and still does."

"And tell me the truth about this maiden, since you have told truly about the knight."

And he told him straightaway everything he had seen and how this maiden killed herself for love of the knight.

"Certainly," said the dwarf, "if she did it it is not surprising, because the knight was among the best in the world and was the son of a king. And know well that by killing him you have brought about your death, because he is from a good lineage and a descendant of such valiant knights that no one but God could save you from death as soon as the truth about his death is told to his family, for they will search for you all over the world until they find you."

"I don't know now," said the knight, "what will come of it, but it grieves me, not for fear of his relatives, but for love of King Arthur whose knight he was."

While the two knights were speaking to the dwarf in this way, out of the forest came King Mark, who later took as wife Iseut the Fair, as this tale will clearly tell, for it is fitting to do so, on account of an adventure the *Book of the Grail* tells about. King Mark had then been recently crowned, was not more than seventeen, and was going to join King Arthur to help him with his war, for all his lands were subject to the realm of Logres. When he arrived at the spot where the two bodies lay on the ground and heard the truth as the two brothers told it, he said he had never heard of a maiden who had loved so faithfully: for her sake and out of respect for her loyalty he would honor both her and her knight.

Then he commanded that his whole retinue dismount, and they did so promptly. He said,

"I want to search throughout this land for a tombstone, the most beautiful and the richest that is to be found, and have it brought here as soon as possible. For be advised that I am one who will not move from this place until they have been buried together in this very spot where they fell dead."

When they heard him speak in this way, they began to search throughout the land in all directions, until they found in a church the stone the king desired. They had it brought to the king, who had already had his tent pitched on the spot, since he wouldn't move until he had done what he set out to do. When he saw that the stone had been brought, he had the bodies very richly buried and the stone erected on top and had carved at the foot of the stone letters which said:

Here lies Lançor, son of the King of Ireland, and at his side Lione his love, who for grief over him killed herself as soon as she saw him dead.

The king had put at the head of the slab a beautiful and rich wooden cross, for it was adorned with gold and silver and various sorts of stones. Thereupon as he was going to leave, it happened that Merlin came by, disguised as an uncouth peasant, and began to write at the top of the stone gold letters which said:

In this place will come together to do battle the two most loyal lovers of their time. And that battle will be the fiercest that had ever taken place before them or will, after them, without a man dying.

When he had done this and carefully inspected the inscription, he began to write in the middle of the stone two names, one, the name of Lancelot du Lac and the other Tristan. And when he had done this, the king, who looked at what he'd done, amazed that so crude and rustic a man could do such a thing, asked who he was.

"King," said Merlin, "I shall not tell you, but you will know it on the day that faithful Tristan is caught with his beloved, and then they will tell you things about me that will displease you."

Then he said to Balain,

"Sir knight, source of great sorrow, why did you allow this maid to kill herself?"

"I was not able," said he, "to move fast enough to take the sword out of her hand to stop her from killing herself."

"You will not be at all so slow," said Merlin, "as you were here, when you strike the tragic blow because of which three kingdoms will be reduced to poverty and desolation for twenty-two years. Know that nothing as dolorous nor as ugly as that blow has been done or ever will be done by any man, for all misery and desolation will come from it. I believe that in you we see Eve, our mother, for, just as through her deeds came the great suffering and misery that we all endure every day, so will be the people of three kingdoms reduced to poverty and desolation by the blow you will strike. And just as He had forbidden her to eat the fateful fruit, so will the Lord have forbidden what you will do. This misfortune will not occur because you are not the best knight in the world at this time, but because you will break the commandment that no one dare break and you will maim the man who is nowadays the most loyal in the world to Our Lord. If you knew how great this misfortune will be and how dearly it will be paid for, you would say that one man has never caused pain in the world like this one that you will bring on, and the day will come when you'll prefer to be dead rather than to have struck that blow."

Then the knight asked him who he was that thus prophesied things to come. Merlin answered,

"You shall not know now but, irrespective of who I am, all this will happen to you."

And Balain answered,

"May God forbid that you speak the truth about this thing. If I thought that a terrible thing such as you tell of were to happen because of me, I would kill myself so as to make a liar out of you and I would be right to do it, because I would be better dead than alive."

After he had spoken, Merlin didn't stay longer, but left for somewhere else so suddenly that King Mark and the others who were there didn't know what happened to him. He hadn't gone far before he met Blaise.[3] He went to meet him and greeted him with great and marvelous joy and said to him,

"Blaise, I'm glad to see you. Now I will acquit myself of the promise I made you in Northumberland, for I have thought a good deal about how you could successfully complete your book. Go to Camelot and wait for me there. When I come back from the defeat of King Rion and from seeing the Accursed Knight perform in that great battle, I will seek you out."

Then Blaise asked him when he thought he would return.

"Within a month," said he, "you'll see me. Do you know where to find me? In Camelot itself."

Then Blaise took leave of Merlin and each one left in a different direction. And now the tale speaks no longer of Merlin or Blaise but returns to Balain and his brother.

Now the tale says that when they were ready to leave, the two brothers went in one direction to find King Rion's army, and

3. A religious man who was the confessor of Merlin's mother and who wrote down Merlin's prophecies and adventures. He is mentioned throughout the *Vulgate* version of the Arthurian romances.

King Mark went toward the city. King Mark asked the knight what his name was. Balaan, who didn't want his brother to be recognized, said to the king,

"Sire, you may indeed know. The two swords that he carries stand for his name. So know that when you hear about the Knight with the Two Swords, it is he."

And the king answered that well he might have that name because he carried two swords.

Thereupon they took their leave and the two knights set out toward the army of King Rion. They hadn't gone far when they overtook Merlin who was walking along, but in a different likeness from the one who spoke to them before. He stopped near them and said,

"Where are you going?"

"What does it matter to you?" said Balain. "How could it profit us if we told you?"

"It could indeed profit you," said Merlin, "so much that if you wanted and dared to undertake what I would tell you, never would such great honor come to two knights as it would to you before tomorrow, for tonight you would be able to achieve what you seek and earn such great honor that it would be talked about forever."

Balain asked him in order to test him,

"How much do you know about what we're out looking for?"

"I know," said he, "that you are seeking to do as much damage to King Rion as is in your power. But whatever you're planning to do will not do you as much good as what I'll show you if you have the courage to do it. Know that between the two of you you have the strength to bring it about easily if you have the courage to follow through."

When they heard these words they were astounded and answered,

"Tell us quickly how we can achieve the great honor which you describe to us. And if we see that it can come about, we'll do exactly as you tell us."

"So," said he, "I will explain to you what I'm referring to. Be advised that King Rion, who is camped near here with his entire host, has arranged to go by night to lie with the wife of the Duke of Vale. Know that he will leave his army to go to the castle where the lady lives as soon as night falls. He will have only forty knights in his company, of whom some will be armed and some not, and over that hill he will come armed in red and mounted on the largest horse of all. You will recognize him by these signs. I have revealed this to you because, if you have the will and the courage to undertake the defeat of the king, I know that you are brave enough men to have the strength to do so if your courage doesn't fail you. No honor has ever come to two knights such as that which will come to you, for know that you will capture the king in such a way that you will be able to take him to King Arthur's prison or to any other place you please."

When they heard these words they were much happier than before. And they said to Merlin,

"How can we believe you about this matter? For if we knew that this could be the truth we would not abandon the task for the whole of the realm, until we had encountered him."

"I will tell you," said Merlin, "what I will do for you. I will accompany you until you are on the road by which the king will come. So that you will trust me more than you trust my words, I will stay with you until I have shown you the king and his company."

And they said that if that were the case, they would go with him, for if he wanted to deceive them and put them in some danger, it would be he who would be the first one to be sorry because he would be the first to die.

"Don't worry," said Merlin, "because as God is my counselor, you will never come to harm through me, nor will any knight who wants to help King Arthur, for without doubt, he is the man in the world whose glory I desire most."

When they heard what Merlin said to them they answered,

"Since you want to come with us, we will follow through as far as we can with what you tell us. But if it happens that the king doesn't come, and that you are lying to us after giving your word, be advised that we will kill you."

"I would be pleased," said he, "to have you kill me if the king doesn't come. But if you fail to take him through your own bungling, I don't want to suffer for it. Now let's go together."

So then they went on their way until they came to a mountain, two of them on horseback and the third on foot. And if Merlin had wanted, one of the brothers would have put him on his horse, but Merlin didn't want to, and said that he would rather go on foot this time. So they went along their way until they came to a high mountain where there were abundant trees, and Merlin led them under the trees and said to them,

"You will stay here until the king comes this way. Have these horses rest and you do the same if you can."

And so they dismounted quickly and took the bridles off their horses and let them go to pasture and they rested as much as they could, but they couldn't rest much, for they had neither food nor drink for the night. And so they waited under the trees until night fell, and Merlin was with them all the while and spoke to them of many things to comfort them. And many times they asked him who he was, and Merlin said to them,

"I am a man such as you can see. Is it your right to ask as long as I show you what I promised to?"

They said that they wouldn't ask any more and Balain kept saying to Merlin,

"You don't seem to me to be an honorable man since you don't dare give us your name."

"Whatever I am," said Merlin, "I'm telling you that after my death people will talk more about my wisdom than about your strength, and yet you are among the best and bravest knights in the world."

Thus the three talked among themselves about many things, and when the moon had risen beautiful and bright, Merlin said to the two brothers,

"Arm yourselves, because the king approaches."

As he spoke these words, they saw a lone squire on a great warhorse pass in front of them, going along at great speed as fast as the horse could carry him. The Knight with the Two Swords asked Merlin,

"Do you know who that is who is going so fast?"

"Yes," said Merlin. "It is a messenger of the king who is going ahead to tell the duke's wife that the king is arriving. Now arm yourselves because he won't be long. And for the sake of God if you were ever a good knight, show it this time, for certainly here you can achieve honor that will never desert you. And if you're lacking courage so that cowardice can invade you, know that nothing can save you from being hewn to pieces and killed. For those who come with the king are not so foolish but that they'll know immediately whether or not you're brave men. I'm telling you this now, handsome lords, so that you can from now on assure peace in the realm of Logres and avenge King Arthur upon the man in this world who is most dangerous to him. And I'm telling you that if you fail now to stop the king you will never again have such a good chance."

"Now don't worry," they said, "for if God please we will certainly get the best of him."

Then they mounted their horses and took their shields and their swords in their hands, and they were in the shadow of the trees so those that passed by on the road couldn't see them. When they had been there for a little while, mounted and armed with their shields and their various weapons and their swords, they heard the noise of horses which had already come up the slope and were appearing on the open space on the mountain. The plateau was at least eight English leagues wide and as long. There was on that plain a forest both beautiful and large which covered most of the mountain. Thus they waited a little bit after they had seen the first of the king's company come along. They approached little by little, since the path up the slope was quite narrow as it went up into the mountain and only one horseman could pass at a time. When there appeared on the hill as many as ten of the king's companions, the two brothers wanted to give their horses free rein because they were anxious to attack them, but Merlin said to them,

"Wait a little bit more so that the king gets up on the mountain, and then we can surprise him for certain because those who are coming with him will thus be easily taken aback."

And they said,

"For God's sake, don't make us wait much longer."

"Don't rush into it yet so soon," said Merlin. "I'll tell you much better when the moment comes than you could possibly know yourselves."

They remained quite silent after he said that. In a few moments, when there must have been as many as twenty-two knights on the mountain, Merlin said to the two brothers,

"Do you remember what I told you this morning about how you can recognize the king? Now you can recognize him easily. We will see now what you do, for now you know that he confronts you."

At this word the Knight with the Two Swords waited no longer and he rushed as fast as the horse would carry him in the direction where he saw the king coming along swiftly, and he shouted at him from far away,

"On guard, king!"

He struck him so hard that he pierced his chest plate because he had no shield. He drove the steel of his sword through his right side so that it came out the other side but he didn't strike him deep enough so that the wound would be mortal. Having attacked with great speed and force, he struck him so hard that he carried him to the ground. The impact was such that the king was shaken up by the fall and fainted from the great pain that he felt and thought he was going to die right on the spot. Balaan, who saw his brother in peril, left the others and ran there where he saw the greatest press of men, and it happened that the first one he ran into was the king's nephew. He struck him so hard with all his strength that he put the steel of his sword through the body and knocked

27

him to the ground so that he couldn't get up because death had already overtaken him. When the brothers had struck their blows they put their hands on their swords and began to strike with vigor left and right, and they knocked down knights and caused horses to stumble. All the others were so amazed by the marvels they saw the two doing that they thought there must be more than a hundred of them. They saw so many of their companions falling one after another from their horses that they thought they couldn't resist much longer. And when the others who were following the king and still climbing up the mountain saw the *mêlée* begin and some of their companions flee and others lying dead and wounded they thought that they must have been ambushed by King Arthur's whole army, so they turned quickly to flee. Seeing no other way out, they rushed down the hill because they thought in that way they could escape. But the slope was so steep and so high that they fled the threat of death to run toward a certain death, for no one who fell down that hill could escape it. Thus the house of King Rion was undone and so many of the forty knights were killed that there were only a dozen left alive besides the king. And these were so broken up with wounds that many of them could not get up again and they were lying on the ground as though dead. And when the two brothers saw that they had so thoroughly undone their enemy, they came to the king to see whether he was dead yet. They unlaced his helmet, took it off his head, and pulled back the hood of his hauberk to catch the wind so that he could get his breath back. When he had been that way for a while and rested a bit, he heaved a great sigh like a man who is coming out of a swoon and opened his eyes, and they said,

"You're dead without possibility of mercy if you don't pledge yourself as prisoner."

They raised their swords and made as if to cut off his head, and when he saw the naked swords that they were menacing him with, he was afraid of dying, so he said to them in haste,

"Ah, good knights, don't kill me! You will gain more by my

living than by my dying. For no profit can come to you from my death but it can from my life, nor is there anything that I would not do to save my life."

"Promise us then," they said, "that you will do what we command you to do."

And he assured them that he would. They swore to him and said that he needn't be afraid of them because they would do him no further harm. They returned to the others who were not grievously wounded and told them they were dead men if they didn't swear to go to prison wherever the two commanded them to. Since they were afraid of dying they promised, and the two brothers reassured them and said that they wouldn't molest them any further. While they were speaking of these things Merlin came up to them and said to the two brothers,

"I want to talk to you a bit. Come over here."

And they went to him and he said to them,

"You came out of this deed quite well. Our Lord has done you great honor, seeing that you have taken a man in as high station as the king by your valor. Now I will tell you what to do if you want to assure yourselves of the affection of King Arthur and of reconciliation with him. You will leave here immediately and take these prisoners with you to the castle of Terrabel. The castle isn't far away and it is your good fortune that you will find King Arthur there and I'm telling you that he has come there this night to rest with his entire host, and I say to you that he is awaiting the morrow to do battle with King Rion with great fear because they have told him that there are a great many more men in King Rion's host than in Arthur's own. For that reason he is not right now sure about the outcome, but he is awaiting the battle with great trepidation. He doesn't have in his company brave enough men to permit him not to fear the news people are bringing him of this tremendous host. Because the army is now so greatly dismayed I am telling you that you could not do anything for King Arthur nor bring him news that would please him more than this will at this very moment."

29

"Now tell us," they said, "whether we will find Arthur where you tell us he is."

"Yes," said Merlin, "and if you hurry you will find that he isn't yet in bed when you get there."

"Now in the name of God," they said, "how lucky we would be if we could find him and speak to him before he retired."

"And if you get there as soon as I do, you will be there sooner than I said."

They said that they certainly would get there in time because they thought they could get there as fast as he could.

"Well then, you'd better come right along, because I'll be there in just a minute."

And he left them.

So the two went to King Rion and his companions and said to them,

"We command you on your oath that you leave immediately from here and we are going to the castle of Terrabel without stopping. And there we will give you over to King Arthur on behalf of us both."

Then Balaan said,

"I don't want this done in behalf of both of us but in behalf of the Knight with the Two Swords."

King Rion said,

"I tell you on my oath that I could in no wise ride without dying of the pain before I get to the castle. So now you can consider that matter."

So they hastily constructed a horse litter to put the king in and then came down from the mountain. When Rion's men came to the plain, they hurried more than was good for them because many of them were badly wounded. They didn't in any way slack their pace for the king's sake because the two brothers were urging them on. In this way, although in great pain, they rode until they came to the castle. When they got to the entrance the two brothers remained outside and said to the guard,

"Good friend, do you see these prisoners we're bringing to

King Arthur? Lead them before the king and watch out that you don't lose one of them, and we will tell you certainly that the king has never had as great a joy as he will have as a result of this deed as soon as he knows who the prisoners are."

The guard said that he would assure them that he would hand the prisoners over to the king.

Merlin, who was already there ahead of them, came to the king and found that he wasn't yet asleep but was conferring in his room with King Mark and four other barons, getting advice on his war. They didn't know exactly what strategy to adopt; they were much too afraid of meeting King Rion in battle because of the news that they had heard about his people. And then Merlin stepped up and said to the king,

"King, I am bringing wondrous and good news to you and all those in the realm, the richest news which has ever come into this realm. Know that the most powerful enemy that you have has been taken and comes at your mercy to be prisoner through the noblest deed you have ever heard spoken of."

The king raised his head and saw that it was Merlin who brought him this news and he asked,

"Tell me Merlin, what enemy is it?"

"It is," said he, "King Rion who has been taken and who is coming here so that you can see him in the hall of your castle."

The king was astonished by this news. He could hardly believe it was true. And he said,

"Can this possibly be true, Merlin, that this has happened as you tell me?"

"Yes, it is true," said Merlin. "You will see him right in front of you in less time than it takes to ride an English league. Then come forth into this hall, you and your barons, and behave in so graceful, dignified, and honorable a way, and let those who are with you behave with such decorum, that King Rion will be amazed when he comes into your presence."

When the king heard that this thing truly happened the way Merlin told it, he was astonished and said,

31

"In the name of God, bless you since you do such an honorable deed for me without my having deserved it."

Then he was joyous and happy and sent word to all the apartments of the castle that all his men should come to him. They came quickly and in such great numbers that the entire hall was full of them, and then soon afterwards the twelve knights of King Rion entered the hall carrying the king on the horse litter. When they entered the hall they began to wail and despair, and they put the litter in the midst of the hall crying all the while. When King Rion saw that he was amongst his barons and knew that before him was King Arthur, he raised up as much as he could because he was grievously wounded and asked which one was King Arthur. Those who were with him told him and he went toward the king at once and knelt before him and said,

"King Arthur, I have been sent as your prisoner by the Knight with the Two Swords who captured me with the help of only one man by means of the greatest exploit that I have ever seen.[4] And I had with me forty armed knights, and all my men were killed by him and his companion except those you see here. I myself would have been killed without mercy if I hadn't sworn to him upon my kingly oath that I would come to you as prisoner. So now I am freed from the oath which I swore to him because I am putting myself in your hands and you can do with me whatever you please, either kill me or let me live."

The king answered that he would not refuse such a prisoner, and then came the others to the fore and did as the king had done and Arthur received them, joyous because of this happening which God had sent to him.

Then King Rion said to him,

"Sire, for God's sake, if you don't want me to die, have me put in some spot where I can rest, somewhere where they will take care of me. I tell you that it is seemly because I am so badly

---

4. In one line the text says that Rion is so severely wounded that he can't move, and in the next he jumps up to go kneel before King Arthur. This is another example of the type of incongruity commonly found in these texts.

wounded that otherwise I will not last long before I die. I have lost
a great deal of blood since I received the wound."

So the king quickly commanded that they take him and his
companions and put them in rooms in the castle and that they send
them physicians who would attend to their wounds. The people
of King Arthur's household did as he commanded. They took
King Rion and his various companions to various rooms. Then
Arthur said to Merlin,

"Do you know who this knight is who has done this good thing
for me—he who has taken prisoner for me as powerful a man as
this king was?"

"Sire," said Merlin, "I know him well. And if you wish I will
tell you who he is."

"And who is he? I'm impatient to know," said the king, "it's
my fondest wish."

"Know then," said Merlin, "that this is the knight who, in your
court, in your own presence did you the great outrage of killing
the damsel. For this you were so angry with him that you
dismissed him from your court."

"Oh, what a sad thing," said the king, "that I sent him away! I
repent of it now, for he has indeed atoned for his sin against the
girl. I would like him to come back to the court now if he wants
to. And if I have said something to displease him, I will make it up
to him in any way he wishes. For it is my belief that he has done
more for me than any mortal knight could do!"

⁵"King," said Merlin, "say no more about it now. You have
said enough. You will never have him in your company again,
whatever happens. But think about something which is of benefit
to you now."

"Say it," said the king, "for I will do nothing unless it be by
your counsel."

"I ask you," said Merlin, "if you are going to do battle with the
army of King Rion?"

5. This is the point at which the passage begins that I have restored to its
original place in the text (see Introduction, p. xvii; and n. 8, p. 59).

"How so?" said the king. "Aren't they going to keep their peace since they know that their lord is in my prison?"

"King," said Merlin, "know this truly: they could in no way believe that you do indeed have him in your prison. And, furthermore, even if they knew it for sure, the king still has a brother, a rich and powerful king whose name is Nero. I tell you that he will cause them to confront you and your men as is fitting for them to do, and for this reason, you must put your affairs in order and prepare yourself well against your enemies, so that they might not surprise you."

The king answered,

"Merlin, I will do nothing unless by your counsel. Now tell us something which can be of use to us because we want to be guided by your advice in everything."

"Now I want to tell you," said Merlin, "about a thing which you might think you could achieve if I didn't warn you, and it is a thing which might cost you all your land."

And the king said,

"We want to take advantage of your counsel in everything."

"I tell you that tomorrow you will have to deal with a company of people who are much to be feared. First, King Rion's soldiers, who, even though they are few, are still more numerous than your men. No doubt, there is no great danger in waiting for them, for they will have little courage as soon as they know what happened to their King Rion, and for this reason, they will be so severely upset because of him that they will be easily defeated; this will happen without doubt. But even though you win over them as you wish, I tell you that then you will have to deal with one who is no less dangerous than King Rion. And do you know who it is? It is King Lot of Orkney, your sister's husband, who is the best knight that you know of all those who wear the crown in your realm. He is quite ill-disposed toward you and has a mortal hatred for you. Do you know why? You know well what a hideous crime you committed against all the children of your land whom you ordered to be brought to you. At the time you had the

34

children taken, your sister, King Lot's wife, had a child. They put
him to sea to send him to you, and whatever happened to the
child, whether he was alive or dead, the king thought in truth that
he had been brought to you and that you had cast him into the sea
like the others. For this reason, they have conceived so great a hate
for you, your sister as well as the king, that they have caused all the
noblemen and good knights of the kingdom of Orkney to assemble, and have had them come to Camelot as though it were to help
you, but this is not true. Rather, it is to harm you; and so we will
see tomorrow, when we engage in battle against the brother of
King Rion, that he and his army will come upon you when the
others are in front of you. This will happen at the same moment.
Now consider what you can do in this predicament, for I have told
you nothing which will not happen just as I've told it to you, with
God as my counsel."

When the king heard what he was threatened with, he was
greatly upset, for King Lot was the man in all his land whom he
feared most. So he said to Merlin:

"I don't know what to say, since King Lot bears me ill will, for
he is the one in all my land in whom I have most confidence in time
of great need and for whom I would do most. And what I did I had
to do in my opinion."

"As things are," said Merlin, "tomorrow you will know the
truth of it."

"Now tell me," said the king, "what we can do. For if they
come up on my rear, and my enemies are in front, the realm of
Logres could be running the risk of losing all honor."

"I will tell you," said Merlin, "what you shall do. You will take
counsel in this matter in the way that I tell you. King Lot is a fine
nobleman and a good knight. One must fear him for many
reasons. Offer your friendship to him first-off, and let him know
that in no way must he fail to defend the realm of Logres as he
should do, and let him take pity on the crown that the honor of the
realm not be sullied because of him. Let him know that you want
him to lead your first column and carry your banner and that he

35

has to uphold the honor of the realm in the way that any loyal man must help to maintain the honor of his lord. Tell him that if you have done something wrong in this world you will make amends for it at his request, as fully as the barons of the realm of Logres shall decide. Let him know all of this right away. And then, when we hear his reply we will consider what to do."

"And where do you think he is?" said the king.

"He is," said Merlin, "near here at a distance of two English leagues with all his army and is only waiting for you to join battle with Rion's men, and then he thinks he can very easily defeat you. Now hurry to tell him what I have told you. You have no time to lose, for King Rion will come soon."

Then the king called two of his knights and requested them to go to King Lot as fast as they could spur their horses and give him his message as best they could. They left the court quickly and went to King Lot's army, and they went straight to the royal tent and saluted him in the name of King Arthur. They gave him the message precisely as it had been given to them and left out nothing as far as they knew. When King Lot heard what Arthur asked, he didn't in any way find his anger diminished, so he answered the messenger:

"Tell your lord that he has not merited my help or any good thing that I might do for him. I will show him as soon as I can that, far from helping him, I must do all in my power to harm him as much as I can."

"How so, sire?" said the messengers, "Will it be thus?"

"Indeed," said he, "will I do my best to take away from him his lands and take his crown from his head because he has quite well deserved it. No man as treacherous as he should wear a crown, in my opinion, since he is guilty of so great a treason as killing the children in his kingdom. If the barons of the realm were as wise as they should be, they would already no longer be calling him lord. They would have killed him and destroyed him as one should do for a traitor and miscreant. Now get out of here! Tell him that he will never find agreement with me until I have avenged my son.

36

He destroyed and put to death undeservedly that tiny creature whom he should have loved as his own flesh. For this I will destroy him, God be willing. And tell him that's how I answer."

They said that they would carry this message, but it afflicted them greatly that they did not find him in better humor. With this they left with the message, mounted and rode until they came to King Arthur, and they told him everything that King Lot had told them. The king was very sad because of this, and more dismayed than he was wont to be. Merlin said to him:

"King, don't be upset, because Our Lord will help you. And know well that he didn't put you in so high a station to snatch you from it so easily without your doing him some grave injury. So ride forth reassured and arrange your people as best you can. I tell you that Our Lord will on this day do you the greatest honor which has for a long time been done to a sinful king. And I want you to make confession of all the things of which you find yourself guilty toward Our Lord. I tell you that this is a thing which will profit you greatly and help you tremendously."

The king did just as Merlin counseled him to. As soon as it was morning, he lined up his men and saw that he had indeed a thousand knights, not to mention soldiers on foot and horseback. Riding around, he arranged ten columns and asked the men if he should go out and wait in that place for the enemy. They argued that he should wait there, for in this way their horses would not be weary from running around over the plain. Thus King Arthur arranged his columns, and then he stopped in the midst of the plain to wait for his enemies to come, and he exhorted his men to do well so that the honor of the realm of Logres would not be tarnished on that day because of them. And they answered him that they would rather die in that very spot than lose honor in the battle. But now the tale no longer speaks of him and his army and goes back to tell about the two brothers who had brought King Rion to King Arthur.

Now the tale tells that when the two brothers had handed over their prisoners into the hands of the gatekeeper, they left Terrabel. They rode toward a hermitage which was about one English league from there. The Knight with the Two Swords knew the hermit quite well, so he called out to him so that the hermit recognized him and opened the door at once. The hermit received him and his brother into his lodging in a very hospitable way and made them comfortable in whatever way he could and gave them bread and water, for he didn't have anything else in his house. That night the two brothers stayed there and rested themselves and their horses, and they made themselves and their horses comfortable with whatever they found in the lodging. They slept until the next day. In the morning when the sun had risen, they got up and had their squires arm them. Then there came a boy who was a relative of the hermit and who said to them:

"I have some news to tell you which is quite astounding. This day near here there will take place the greatest battle that has ever been in the realm of Logres. King Arthur and the men of King Rion will join in pitched battle presently, on a plain nearby."

"Are you sure?" said the knight.

"Yes," said he, "because I have seen their banners flapping in the wind. Now let Our Lord come to the aid of King Arthur, because certainly it would be too painful a loss if he were defeated."

So they drew aside and consulted each other on what they could do and Balaan said:

"Sire, if it pleases you, how would you like us to go to this battle?"

"I want us to go where this battle is to be," said Balain.

"When we see that the brother of King Rion is engaged in this battle, we will attack him. If indeed it befell us by the will of Our Lord or by something else that we can surprise his men, I doubt if he will escape us very easily without first agreeing to our terms. If by the grace of God we capture him for Arthur, I will then have made my peace with Arthur and have his friendship and affection, as I did before I killed the maiden."

38

So they were quite agreed on this matter and went up to the hermit, took leave of him, and left quickly. They went in the direction of the place they knew the battle was supposed to be. They had hardly been going long before they saw the entire countryside covered with armed knights. In one direction and the other flags and richly beautiful banners of various colors were blowing in the wind. Nero, the brother of King Rion, had already received news that his brother was captured, but he had hidden it so well from the men in his army that none of them knew the truth, except his first cousin, who had told him about it. In the morning when the great barons of the army asked where the king was, he told them:

"Ride in confidence, because between him and me, we will lead the first column and the last. Don't be dismayed because you will not strike a single blow without his being there."

In this way, Nero had arranged his columns and made ten just as Arthur had done. But there were a lot more people on his side than there were on the side of King Arthur. When he had arranged them the best he knew how, he sent forth the first three, and you could see when the two armies came together lances breaking, knights falling, and horses running wild, far and near, for there was no one to hold them back, since each one had too much to attend to.

Those who were on King Arthur's side, however, weren't so numerous, and they suffered and endured a great deal at the beginning. If they hadn't been as noble and as good knights as they were, they would have been easily defeated. They were, however, agile, quick, and of a good age, and young men, all of them, prepared to die rather than lose honor in the battle. These were the things that enabled them to do so well on that day when there were so many killed and wounded. When the lances were broken, they were taking up their swords on all sides, and then began *mêlées*, so mortal and dangerous that in a very short time you could see the whole place covered with dead and wounded knights. Nevertheless, through their own efforts, King Arthur's men were winning the day. When defeat turned upon the men of King Rion so that the first three columns were forced to turn tail, Arthur's men, with all their power, struck the others who had come to help them. Those troops formed three columns all in a line dressed in steel and well armed.

In this battle King Arthur brought down many men and there were many wounded and maimed, for there were all too few standing against the attackers and they might well have perished quickly on the spot; no sooner was one caught than he was hacked to pieces. King Arthur sent three well ordered and well armed columns to help them. Then they held rather well. There were, nonetheless, many more on King Rion's side than on King Arthur's. In this way all the columns from both sides met so that when one group was doing badly, their companions would come quickly to their aid. When the two brothers saw that King Arthur was not in the column, they said:

"We have waited too long. Now to our enemies! We have left them in peace too long."

Then they faced the last column, the same one Nero was in, and went toward the thickest part of the fight, meeting in their path two knights who were considered to be very brave. They struck them in the body with their lances. Neither shield nor armor could protect them from the steel, and the brothers knocked them from their horses in such condition that they needed no physician because they were mortally wounded and as they fell they broke both the lances. The brothers took hold of their swords and began to rain great blows on all around them. Knocking down and killing knights, they tore helmets from heads and shields from around necks. The two of them accomplished such feats of arms against their enemies that anyone who saw them would have been amazed. If anyone asked me which sword the Knight with the Two Swords used in the battle, I would answer that it was his own and not the one that had belonged to the damsel. For he never used that sword before the day when he took the field against his brother Balaan and killed him with it because he didn't recognize

40

him, and when his brother killed him with the same one. As Robert de Boron will tell before the second part of his book.

Great was the battle that day in the plain before Terrabel. That day King Arthur did much; wounded and maimed many to clearly show his enemies the virtue of his good sword Excalibur. Those it so finely cut paid dearly, for he killed with his own hand and his own sword, by the time the battle was ended, more than twenty knights and wounded more than forty. Kay the Seneschal in his turn did very well for himself and accomplished so much during that day that he was heaped with praise and honor that lasted a long while after. Hernil de Rivel, who in those days was a rather young knight, did very well also. But no deed that either he or anyone else accomplished on that day was praised as much as what was done by the Knight with the Two Swords, for he accomplished feats of knightly prowess that were so outstanding that wherever he went everyone looked at him with amazement and said that he was no mortal knight but some monster or devil that ill luck had brought there. King Arthur himself, when he had watched him carefully and had seen the marvels that he accomplished, said that he was not a knight like any other, but some man born just to destroy people. It was to Gifflet that he said this and it has been repeated far and wide.

Thus was the battle joined and fought by both sides. So Merlin went to King Lot and found that he was preparing his men as best he could to attack King Arthur. Then Merlin said to him:

"Oh King Lot, up until now you've been a very loyal man toward your rightful lord. Now you are acting like a person who is abandoning good works near the end of his life. Up until now you have been loyal, and now as you approach your death you want to become disloyal and show your disloyalty openly to the people. Now look! How can you commit so great a treachery as to fail him in his need when he is fighting for you and his people and putting himself in danger in order to save you and all the others from being subjected by foreign princes? And in the midst of this peril you are preparing another for him! In the same place where he's offering himself to defend you from your enemies you are preparing to kill him if you can. Look now whether this is not treachery and crime?"

"Merlin," said the king, "if I hate him it is no wonder. He has indeed, recently committed the greatest treachery that ever a king has done and has done evil to all the good men of this realm. And he has deprived me of an heir that God himself had sent me and didn't care at all that it was my son, I who was the most prominent man in his realm. I was such a good friend to him that I had his sister as wife so that my child was his nephew. Now see if his crime wasn't treacherous!"

"Now tell me," said Merlin, "do you think that he killed your child?"

"Yes," said the king, "I know that it is true. He put him to sea with the others. For this reason I shall never want nor ever desire that there be love nor agreement of any kind between him and me, but war all the rest of the days of my life."

"King," said Merlin, "you are wrong, you should not say something that is not true. Know that Mordred is alive. If you want to hold off on what you have begun just now, I promise you that I'll show him to you healthy and alive within two months."

"I will believe no one at all," said the king, "no matter what they say until I've seen him."

"And what're you going to do about it?" said Merlin.

"I won't move a step unless to go to war. There I will avenge myself if I'm not prevented from it by death."

"And I am saying to you," said Merlin, "that if you are so hasty as to go to war, I tell you that you'll be dishonored because of it. You'll be defeated and will be captured and many of your men killed. You'd better believe what I'm telling you, for you've never heard tell that I speak lying words which I claim to be truth. You'll be sorry if you don't do what I tell you."

The king said that no man would prevent him from facing danger to seek vengeance.

"May you succeed," said Merlin, "but it is certain that you will repent at a time when you won't be able to make amends, and this repentance will come too late. It will be a great catastrophe."

While Merlin was speaking in this way to the king, there were several barons nearby and each one of them was saying to the king:

"Ah, sire, for God's sake, do what Merlin is telling you to, because his counsel has never resulted in evil for you or for any man."

And the king kept saying that in no case would he do anything of the kind.

Merlin knew quite well that at that moment King Arthur was fighting and that if it happened that King Lot fell upon him just then, the slaughter would be great. He held the king under the sway of his words as long as he could and forced him to listen and prevented him from advancing. He didn't want Arthur to stop fighting, at least until he had beaten King Rion's men. For this reason, Merlin caused King Lot to stay there until the hour of terce. He held him in such a way that he didn't ride any farther away than over four acres of land, and all of this he did by enchantment, until he could see what would result from the battle. He helped King Arthur so much all that time, for he would rather King Arthur be healthy and strong and that King Lot be killed. He knew that one of them would die if they joined battle together.

Just after the hour of terce, a messenger came to King Lot and said to him:

"Sire, I bring terrible news. King Arthur has beaten King Rion's men. No one has ever seen as great or thick a battle as that one was, for there were very many people killed on both sides. In fact, so many prisoners were taken by the king that there must have been more than five hundred of them, all important men, I think."

When the king heard this tale, he was quite amazed, and looked around to see if he could see Merlin, because he wanted to cut off Merlin's head since he now realized that he had cast a spell on him and had delayed him, at his will. Then he said to his men:

"Merlin has undone me. If I had ridden out this morning I would have defeated the king and won my quarrel. I'm further away from it now than I ever was before, and as long as I live I will never again have the king in as good a position as I had him this morning. Now I don't know what to do. If I go to him he will have me seized as his mortal enemy because I would not do what he asked me to, and if I go back to my lands he will gather his men and come with his host to attack me and destroy both me and my country. If I conquer him he will have no more mercy from me than I would have had from him, so I don't know what to decide. I can't see escape for me anywhere."

Then one of his knights, who was his first cousin, answered him:

"Sire, you will not receive mercy from the king unless you exact it with the steel blade. Attack him, for Our Lord will give you success in the battle."

"Very well," said the king, "I wish to go nowhere save to battle." Then the king asked the messenger:

"Does King Arthur have a lot of men with him?"

"Truly not," said the young man, "they're almost all wounded and the best of them are completely exhausted from this battle which they've just won."

"Well then, let's go," said the king, "and make sure that you all perform so marvelously that when you arrive, not one of them remains in his saddle."

They said that they were all ready, since it was the king's pleasure. So they didn't delay any longer, but put their columns in order and went along their way straight toward King Arthur's army.

Merlin had already gotten back to the king. He found him wounded in more than eight places. Some wounds were small and some were large, and he saw that the king's men were disarming him so that he could be more at ease, for they didn't think that he would have to fight that day. And then Merlin said to the king:

"O king, take up your coat of mail and don't disarm because

44

you have more to do than you think. You see, King Lot of
Orkney and all of his barons are coming with a host against you.
You can already see their banners up on that mountain and their
standards raised on high, advancing rapidly toward you."

"O God," said the king, "what a curse! You are sending me
these trials because of my sins. Now I think that all these good men
are going to pay for what I have done wrong against you."

When the barons heard these words, there wasn't one that
didn't pity him in his heart. And they answered:

"King, don't be dismayed, but ride in confidence, for Our Lord
will lead you and will make you successful against your enemies in
such a way that you will have victory and they will all have
dishonor."

Then one of the knights of the king's company spoke, and it was
he that had so long hunted the Strange Beast, he who had later
engendered Perceval, so the tale will tell quite in full. He had done
so well in the battle on that day, that no one had done better except
the Knight with the Two Swords and his brother.

"Sire," said he to the king, "do not be dismayed about this, for
you should know that you will win." And the king answered:

"Sir knight, thank you for having helped me so staunchly.
Now know that all my faith is in God and in you and in the other
good men. And indeed if it were up to you and other knights such
as you, I know truly that it would not last very long, and I beg of
you tell me who you are because I don't know you by the armor
that you are wearing."

"I will hide it from you no longer," said he, "I'm the knight
whom you saw chasing the Strange Beast. Because of the good-
ness I know is in you I came to help you, not because I hold a
kingdom from you—you know that well."

"Indeed," said the king, "you will hold one from me whenever
you wish for you have well deserved it."

When they had arranged their columns, they set out toward
King Lot's men. When the two armies came together, you could
see a greater slaughter of knights and more dying people than

anyone had ever seen before, for there were good knights on both sides and they attacked each other in such a deadly way that at the first shock you could see hundreds lying on the ground with their armor torn from their bodies.

That battle was without doubt so cruel and wicked that it began at the hour of terce and lasted until the hour of vespers. If King Lot had not been as good a knight as he was, his men would have been undone long before they were. All alone he bore the brunt of the battle which was all around him, so that all who saw him crossed themselves, amazed that he could withstand the half of what was being inflicted upon him. He accomplished all manner of brave deeds and tasks in front of all those who dared to approach him. Thus there was no one, however brave, near him who, having watched him, would not be awed by his blows. When King Arthur saw this marvel and had recognized that it was indeed King Lot, he said:

"Ah, God, what a shame that such a brave man as he is doing such evil deeds! According to the prowess which I see in him, it is my opinion that he is indeed worthy of having the entire world in his sway."

King Lot was striving for no less than to be able to kill King Arthur. He charged ahead, sword drawn, like one who was intent only on the king's death. And when King Arthur saw him coming, he wasn't prepared to receive him. So he pulled his bridle back and threw up his shield to receive the blow. Lot, who had aimed his blow, almost touched the king, and he struck the horse on the forward saddle bow. The sword was strong and sharp, the blow was swung in a high arc, and King Lot was strong, so he struck the horse hard and sliced him through between the shoulders, so that the horse fell dead on the ground and the king flew over his neck. Then the Knight of the Strange Beast thought that the king was dead, and he was very sad and said that this was a great pity because the people of the realm of Logres would never again see as noble a king as he was.

"I will avenge him if I can," said he.

46

Then he charged at King Lot with his sword drawn. When the latter saw him coming, he did not turn away. He waited for him resolutely and without his shield, because it had just fallen to the ground on the same spot. And the knight hit him so hard that neither his helmet nor his iron headpiece could prevent him from being split to the shoulder. The blow he struck caused King Lot to fly onto the ground. And when the men of Orkney saw this blow, they were so amazed that they didn't know what to do, because he in whom they had faith to lead them in the battle, if the battle was ever to be won, was dead. When King Arthur's men saw him dead, he who throughout the day had caused more damage and destruction than half of his troops had, they were more reassured than they ever had been, and they ran upon the men of Orkney and killed and knocked them down and reigned destruction among them as best they could. They were so disarrayed that they couldn't stand it for long, so they turned their back and fled the place at great speed and galloped off as fast as their horses could go, like men who thought only to save their lives, for they saw that defeat had come their way. King Arthur's men followed them because they hated them so mortally, and they sliced them and killed them in such great numbers that the road was covered with them wherever they passed. And that is how the men of Orkney were undone.

The were defeated, and Pellinor killed King Lot of Orkney. All the latter's sons, when they became knights, so hated Pellinor and all his family that Gawain later killed Lamorac, Driant, and Agloval in the quest of the Holy Grail, as Sir Robert de Boron will tell fully in his book. But if Perceval the good knight who was the brother of Agloval had known about Agloval's death, he would have, without doubt, avenged him, because he loved Agloval more than any brother ever loved another.[6]

6. This paragraph has been reconstructed from the four versions: the Cambridge MS, the Huth MS, and the editions by Bonilla and Bohigas of the Spanish translations of the text. The matter will be treated in detail in the critical edition of the text now in preparation (cf. Introduction, pp. xviii–xix).

When the battle had been won so completely that of all the men of Orkney there wasn't one left who wasn't either dead or captured, the king had all the dead knights assembled and had the bodies of all buried together on a rocky hill which was very high, and on it he had a church built so that people should pray for the souls of those who were buried there. They didn't have such a great ceremony for the other bodies, but they buried them all in the woods and in the fields.

And in King Rion's attack it happened that all twelve kings were killed.[7] King Arthur had their bodies taken and put into the Church of St. Stephen of Camelot and had each name written down. But for King Lot, whom he loved well, he organized a great ceremony and had him put in a beautiful and rich tomb. In his honor he had a church built on the very spot which was of great worth and will be as long as the world shall last, and that church was named the Church of St. John.

The queen, Lot's wife, and his four sons, who were handsome children, came to bury him, and they all mourned deeply, for they all loved him well. King Urien came and Morgan his wife, so pregnant that she was on the point of having a child. She was an evil and malicious woman and knew a great deal about gossip and evil thoughts. When the king had been buried, Gawain, his oldest son, who was certainly a handsome child and was at that time only eleven years old, mourned so piteously that all who saw him had great pity for him. When he had wept for his father in such a way that no man of his age could have done better, he spoke a word which was heard clearly and not forgotten and that word was this:

"O my lord, he has done me painful injury, King Pellinor who has killed you, and he has impoverished and debased our lineage by your death, and even the kingdom of Logres itself is deprived more than it would have been by the loss of seven of its best kings.

7. These are the twelve rebel kings mentioned in the *Vulgate Merlin* whom Arthur had to defeat in order to establish his rule in Britain. The scribe apparently sees no need for explanation, assuming that all readers are familiar with the earlier work.

Now let it not please God that I accomplish any praiseworthy deed of chivalry until I have exacted the vengeance for such a thing that one must, that is, to kill a king for a king."

And Gawain knew well that it was King Pellinor who had killed his father, and all those who heard it were amazed by this oath because it was indeed very solemn, even coming from such a child as was Gawain at that age. Those who heard it said:

"This child has spoken a noble thing; he will indeed avenge his father someday."

He did just as he said he would. For later, he killed King Pellinor and two of his children.

King Arthur, who was very pleased with the outcome of the affair which Our Lord had granted him, said that for a week from that day he would celebrate the victory. Then he had made twelve kings of metal which were richly plated with silver and gold and had a golden crown placed on the head of each one and had each one's name written on his chest, and at the same time he had made a statue of a king in the image of King Lot which looked as much like him as could be accomplished. After that he had built another statue of a king ten times richer than all the others and had it made in the image of himself. When all these images were ready, the thirteen of them made in such a manner that each one held a candlestick in his hand, the one which was made to look like King Arthur held in his hand a naked sword in such a posture that he seemed to be threatening the others. When all this work was done the king had the statues put in the main tower of the castle high on the battlements so that everyone in the city could see them clearly, and each king held a large lighted candle. In the middle of the twelve statues was that of King Arthur, quite a bit taller than the rest of them, holding its sword in its hand so that it seemed to be threatening all those around him. All the others around his statue seemed to be bowing before it as though they were asking mercy for some ill deed.

When this had been done, as I have told you, the celebration which lasted eight full days began inside Camelot. The first day

49

after it had begun, King Arthur looked around and said to Merlin who was near him:

"Merlin, it seems to me that it would be a marvelous thing if those candles could keep burning so that they wouldn't go out by night or day, even if it rained or blew."

"Indeed," said Merlin, "I will cause them to last longer than you would dare to think."

So then he cast his spell, and said to the king:

"King, know that these candles will not go out until my soul leaves the body, and the day on which they go out two miracles will happen in this land. I will be delivered unto death by the conniving of a woman, and the Knight with Two Swords will strike the dolorous stroke in defiance of Our Lord's injunctions as a result of which the adventures of the Holy Grail will begin, in particular in the kingdom of Logres. Then will begin to take place painful and calamitous events across all of Great Britain, and these will happen so often that those who see will be amazed and all that will last twenty-two years."

"Merlin," said the king, "in view of this prophecy which you've told me may I know whether the day on which you will die is near or far?"

"Truly you will know," said Merlin, "the day when the adventures begin in this way: these candles will go out then, and there will be a great darkness upon the land in the middle of the day and no one will see a thing at the hour of noon. At that moment it will so happen that you will be hunting and will have got off your horse near a fountain to kill a beast and the darkness will come upon you so that you won't know what happened to your game, and I tell you that at that moment, you will not be without great doubt and great fear."

The king was amazed at all of this business, so he said to Merlin:

"Merlin, can you tell me when this will happen?"

"You will not know it from me," said Merlin, "nor from anyone else."

And the king let it go at that, but he asked him on the other hand:

"Tell me what happened to King Pellinor and what happened to the two brothers who were so valorous in the battle. I've had them searched for far and near and they are not to be found. They have done so much for me that I will not be at ease until I have rewarded them within my power to do so."

"I tell you," said Merlin, "that you will not see the two brothers again as soon as you think, and when you see them it will not be a happy occasion, because they will do you harm by mistake."

So that day they spoke of many things, and finally Merlin said to the king:

"King Arthur, I will not stay much longer with you, but one thing more I will say which you would like to know if you are wise. Guard the scabbard of your sword well, for I tell you that you will never again find so marvelous a one if you lose it. Do not put it in the hand of any person whom you do not completely trust, for if it is recognized, you will never get it back, and you certainly saw well, the day before yesterday, how valuable the scabbard was, because you received several wounds in the battle, but from none of them did you lose any blood."

"I will keep it," said the king, "as well as I can."

And on that day King Rion paid homage to King Arthur and was granted his lands by the latter. King Arthur established him as king over all the realms which were within his purview, and they spoke to each other about the candles which burned thus.

When Morgan found out that Merlin had done this by enchantment, she thought that she would get close to him and learn enough of what he knew so that she could do some of the things she wanted, wherever she wished.

So then she got to know Merlin and asked him if he would teach her what he knew in return for which she would do anything he asked of her. When he saw that she was so beautiful, he fell deeply in love with her and said:

"Lady, why would I hide something from you? You could ask nothing of me which I would not accomplish as well as I can."

"Sire, I give you my heartfelt thanks," said she, "I will indeed see whether it's true, because now I'm asking you to teach me enough about casting spells that there would be no woman in this land who knows more than I."

And he said that he would certainly teach her. And so he taught her so much in a very short time, because she was receptive, clever, and eager to learn, that she knew a great part of what she wanted. The science and art of magic pleased her very much.

Then when her time came she was delivered of a male child, whom they called at baptism, Yvain, and he became later a famous knight of great prowess and great strength.

When she had learned as much magic as she had wanted to, she chased Merlin from her presence because she saw clearly that he loved her with a passionate love, and she told him that she would cause him great dishonor if he lingered longer at her side. He was very sad because of this, but he didn't want to do the wrong thing because he loved King Arthur well, and so he left her presence as soon as he could.

In the realm there was a knight who was a very handsome man and who was very brave and strong of body, whom she loved with a noble love and he her. They frequented each other so much that he had carnal knowledge of her, and this affair pleased the lady so much that she loved him above all other men. She went right away to the king's lodging and the king believed in her more than in any other thing in the world. And because of the faith that he had in her, he charged her to watch over Excalibur and said to her repeatedly:

"For the sake of God, guard it for me and watch closely over the scabbard more than anything else, for it is the accessory which I am most fond of in this world and which I must guard most closely."

When she heard this thing, she was amazed that this could be, and she told it to the knight that she loved, and when he heard of it he answered:

"I beg of you, if you have ever loved me, find out why he holds this scabbard so dear, for it is certainly not without reason."

"I will find out for you," she said, "as soon as I can."

One day she asked the king about it. He believed in her so much that he told her straightaway why he valued the scabbard so much.

"By my faith," said she, "you have now told me enough that never any man will have it in his hands except you. Now I will guard it much more carefully than I did before."

In the evening her friend came back and she told him right off everything the king had told her.

"By my faith," said he, "since it has such great power, I want to have it."

"I'm quite willing," said she, "but wait until I have a scabbard made which looks like it both in construction and appearance, because if I give it to you now and the king asks for it later and I cannot show it or another one like it to him, he will undo me on the spot."

"Then make haste," said he, "because I won't rest easy until I have it."

Then Morgan commanded that a man come to her who was skilled in such works, and she commanded him to make another one like it. He looked at it and said that he would do it, but only if he could have the model before him all the time. Morgan installed him in one of the rooms of the apartment so that the scabbard wouldn't be far away, and the man worked there until he had made a copy of it. The two of them were so much alike there couldn't have been three men in the world who could tell them apart. When the workman had done this and Morgan saw that everything was indeed done to perfection, she was afraid that he would betray her in some way, that the king would kill her when he knew the truth, so she had the man's head cut off and had his body thrown into the sea. Then she sent for her friend to come to speak to her and he did. And when he was in her room and was looking at the scabbards, one and the other, it so happened that King Arthur who had just been hunting entered the hall. They were surprised and afraid. They suspected that if the king found them alone together it might go badly for them, so they fled, one in one direction and the other in another, into various rooms of the castle, and left the scabbards on the bed, one on top of the other, and the swords on the carpet. The door of the room was closed so that no one could enter. The king entered his room and found Morgan, who had arrived before him. When she had been with him for quite awhile, she went back where she'd been before and then looked at the scabbards and to her dismay couldn't tell them apart because they were so much alike. So then it happened as it pleased God that she took the genuine scabbard and put the sword in it, but she thought she was doing the opposite, so she gave to her friend the second one and said to him:

"Now you have the one whose virtue cannot be lightly dismissed. I'm giving it to you."

So he accepted the scabbard which he thought had marvelous virtues and took it away with him. That very week it happened that he fought a knight who was his enemy whom he met in the forest, and it happened that the thing in which he had the most confidence did not help him at all, nor was it worth anything; thus he was so much wounded in this battle and so much blood did he lose that he almost died. But in any case he escaped as well as he could and came back to his lodging so wounded and maimed that he could hardly stay in the saddle. He was very upset about this happening because he thought that he could have won at his leisure, and so he decided that he would be avenged if he could, but he didn't see how he could do it without revealing all to King Arthur. So he meditated about how he could reveal it somehow in such a way that the king would blame no one except Morgan.

One day the king went hunting in a great and deep forest. It happened that the knight was following him nearer than any of the others, and it happened that the king was separated from all of his company except the knight, and when he had hunted as much as he pleased, he went back accompanied by the knight and they began to speak of many things. And after a while the knight said:

"Sire, I would tell you something if I could be sure that misfortune would not befall me because of it. Know that I'm telling it to you for your benefit and advantage."

"Speak," said the king, "for no misfortune will happen to you because of it but all good things if I see that my honor is involved."

"Sire," said the knight, "I beg your forgiveness for a thing which I had arranged to your detriment, and I'll tell you what it is. In truth Morgan your sister hates you and I don't know why, but that hate is so deep that she is pursuing your death in any manner that she can. For this reason she asked me to come and see her the day before yesterday and made me swear on the saints that I would do everything that she asked me. And when I had sworn the oath she said to me, 'I want you to avenge me in such a way that you kill him without delay.' And I answered, 'Lady, I cannot do this without dying.' 'Don't worry about that,' she said, 'because I will give you an accessory, which, as long as you carry it, will prevent you from losing a drop of blood or receiving a mortal wound.' Then she gave me the scabbard of a sword and said, 'I'm giving this to you and it will serve you in the way that I've explained. Know that if you avenge me upon my brother as I told you, I will make you a very rich man for all the days of your life.' Sire, this is the manner in which your sister spoke to me. But since I am your liege man, I must not seek to do you harm no matter what happens. I admit this to you and I beg of you to watch out for her and know well that she hates no one as much as she hates you."

Hearing these words and this extraordinary disclosure, the king crossed himself and asked that the knight give him the scabbard.

"Now give me the scabbard and know that I will avenge myself quite fairly for this treachery."

He gave him the scabbard thinking that he had done his duty well. So the king went straight back to the castle where he had left Morgan. But Merlin, who by his tricks and enchantments knew what the king had said to the knight, when he saw the king was returning in such a hurry to the castle, knew that he would immediately slay Morgan if she weren't quickly removed from his path. He loved Morgan quite deeply and so he had it arranged that she could hide with him. He went to her quickly and said:

"You are condemned and shamed."

And then he told her everything about the knight and the king. When she heard what had happened, she was quite afraid that the king would have her put to death, and she begged Merlin for mercy and fell on her knees in front of him and said to him:

"Oh Merlin, have mercy upon me and help me in this time of need, for otherwise will I be shamed, and certainly you know that I've never said such a thing to the knight as that of which he has accused me to the king."

"How can I help you?" said Merlin.

"I will tell you how," she said. "You stay here and I'll get on my horse and leave the castle and pretend that I'm running away. When the king comes and asks about me, you explain to him that someone stole the sword and scabbard from me and that I was greatly afraid of staying here because of the fear I had of my brother. In that way the knight will be dishonored."

Merlin said that he would indeed do this for love of her, so she had one of her horses saddled quickly and brought in the scabbard which she was keeping so that the king wouldn't find it and left the castle all alone without company.

After this it wasn't long until the king came out of the woods and rejoined his company. When he came he asked right away where Morgan his sister was, so Merlin stepped right up and said to the king:

"Sire, everything is going badly. She left your lodging and has gone off to her own land."

"And why has she left?" said the king.

"Sire, because by some misfortune that I don't understand someone has stolen from her the scabbard of a sword which you had given her to keep and which you had told her to guard well above everything else. So she has lost it through the treachery of some knight who was in her company, and she was so afraid of your anger that she didn't dare wait for you to arrive, so she left."

When the king heard this he fell immediately into new

thoughts and he thought then that the knight had stolen the scabbard and that he had said all that he did out of hate for Morgan, so he was quite angry and looked angrily at the knight and said to him:

"Aha, sir knight, you have come close to causing me to commit the greatest outrage that a king has ever committed. For if I had found my sister right away I would have killed her because of your words. But now I know that you were lying in everything that you told me."

So he drew his sword and said to him:

"Here is your payment for the false message," and struck him a great blow which caused his head to fly off for more than the length of a lance away from the body. Then he said to Merlin:

"Where do you think my sister is?"

And Merlin told him. Then the king sent people after her as fast as they could spur, and those who were searching for her found her in a nunnery and brought her to the king. When he saw her he gave her back the scabbard and said to her:

"Now watch over this better than the last time, for chance has brought it back to me. And if I had found you here I would have made you pay dearly."

The king still believed that the scabbard he held was the one which was given him with the sword. So by her cleverness Morgan made peace with her brother whose death she was scheming for as best she could. The king didn't see that she was planning anything evil and for that reason he kept her near him.

King Urien went very often to Arthur's court because he loved his wife who had been there day and night for many days. Because she was so discerning in many things, King Arthur loved her a great deal, but later he hated her mortally, as the tale tells, and rightly so because she tried to have him killed. King Urien had a cousin who was a handsome lad and proud and so wise for his age that everyone was amazed by it, and there was no young man in those days in the realm of Logres who was so well endowed, for he was handsome and brave and gracious. The young man was seventeen years old, about ready to receive the honor of knight-hood. King Urien loved nothing in the world as much as he loved him, and he usually called him Baudemagus. He went usually with the son of King Lot whom they called Gawain and with Gahariet his brother, and he liked to be in the company of no one as much as he enjoyed theirs, for he was only six years older than Gawain.

One day the young man was eating in the palace. The king had already eaten and they were going around, all three of them, enjoying themselves in the castle. Baudemagus was in the middle and had his right arm around Gawain and his left around Gahariet. The three of them came in this way to Merlin, and he looked at them and began to be angry and upset and he said, loud enough so that several nearby could hear him:

"Ah, Baudemagus, at your right is the one who will cause your death; it's such a shame, for in this country no wiser prince will die within your lifetime than you."

Several people heard this prophecy and they didn't understand it very well because they didn't know anything about things to come. And King Arthur asked that Merlin repeat what he had just said, but he didn't want to, so those who heard it told it to the king just as they'd heard it. The king had it written down quickly and he didn't know what it meant, but later he understood this pro-phecy very well because he then knew in truth that Sir Gawain had killed Baudemagus.

Everyone in the castle was talking much about Baudemagus to such an extent that Sagremor's father, the same who had had Mordred raised with his son and who was with King Urien and had come to court on that day, said to King Urien:

"Sir, you should rejoice greatly at having raised someone as well as you have Baudemagus, for indeed I don't know these days of any young man in this country who is as worthy as he is, and let it please God that I might have an heir such as he, for certainly I would prize him highly."

"In the name of God," said King Urien, "I love him so much

that I couldn't love him more if he were my son, and I love him more for the good that I see in him than I would for being mine."

At these words Merlin came forward and said to Sagremor's father:

"King Urien can rejoice over his guardianship more than you can yours and will do so, for he will see his foster child turn out well and you will see yours cause you to die one day by a sharp cutting sword. One of these here will kill the other so that you can say that you have put the wolf with the lamb, and thus the one will rejoice in the death of the other. And that day you will see that a deadly battle will take place on the plain of Salisbury when the high chivalry of the realm of Logres will be turned to death and destruction."

At these words they were all amazed, so they told it right away to the king and the king answered:

"These are Merlin's prophecies. Put them down with the others."

And so they did what he commanded, and then the king said to Merlin:

"Merlin, tell me if these things that you're saying within my hearing will happen within my time."

"Yes, in truth," said Merlin, "I'm not speaking obscure words whose meaning you will not know before you leave this world."

And the king said that he agreed that it should be so.[8]

The next day, around the hour of noon, when the king had had his camp set up on a field outside the castle and when his tent had been erected on a path amongst some bushes, he felt a bit tired and went to lie down in his tent. He commanded that everyone leave except his servants. He began to think about a thing which displeased him a great deal. Thinking this way he was as sad as anyone could be. For that reason he could not lie down and rest. While he was plunged in this train of thought, he listened and heard the hoofbeats of a horse which was coming along the road at great speed, neighing and making the biggest noise in the world.

8. This is the end of the restored passage (cf. n. 5, p. 33).

The king jumped out of his bed to go see what was going on and rushed out of his tent and found that all of his personal servants were asleep. And he saw that a knight was coming from the direction of the castle of Meliot, fully armed and mourning as bitterly as anyone could and saying to himself:

"O God, what have I done to deserve to be the cause of such great misfortune and suffering? I don't see what I can do. I was never in the habit of committing such acts of treachery."

And when he had said this he began wailing again as much or more than he had before.

When he arrived before the king, the king said to him:

"Ha, sir knight, I beg you in the name of chivalry to tell me why you are carrying on such great mourning."

And the knight answered:

"Sire, I will tell you nothing because you can in no way rectify it."

And he passed along without saying any more.

When the king saw that he would learn no more, he was very unhappy and said to himself:

"Ah, Lord God, I am very sad because I don't know why this knight is in such pain."

The knight went along at top speed on his way, straightaway toward a mountain.

The king watched him go as long as he could and said:

"Ah, God, it is great affliction that I do not know that knight's secret."

While he was looking in that direction it wasn't long before he saw coming down the road the Knight with the Two Swords, the knight whom he valued the most at that time because of his feats of arms, and he came straight up to him and when the knight saw the king he went over to meet him and said:

"Sire, I am ready to do whatever I can in this world for you."

"You have indeed shown me that not long ago," said the king. "But now I am asking you to do something for me which will certainly not put you out very much in my opinion."

And the knight said to him that even if it did him injury he would attempt to do it because the king had requested it.

"I beg of you," said the king, "that you follow a knight who has just gone by here."

And he showed him the direction in which the knight had gone.

"Arrange either amicably or by any other means that he come here to me and know that I don't desire this to cause him any harm, but I would like to know, if he agrees, why he was going by here just now carrying on such great mourning."

"Sire," said the Knight with the Two Swords, "thank you, if it may please you, because you are asking me to do it I will willingly go and bring him back to you, God willing."

Then he mounted his horse, left the king, and went at top speed after the knight. He hadn't ridden far when he saw him ahead and he and his horse were both wearing white, and the Knight with the Two Swords hurried as fast as he could gallop and caught up with him at the foot of a mountain. Beside him was a damsel who was saying to him:

"Why are you mourning? If you weren't doing it someone else would."

And he answered:

"It would have been much better for me to die ten years ago than to have to undertake this adventure."

And all the while he kept up his wailing.

And then the Knight with the Two Swords came up to him and said:

"Sir, may God be your guide."

And the other answered that God should bless him.

"Good gentle sir," said the Knight with the Two Swords, "I would like to ask you for the sake of God and the sake of chivalry that you come back a bit so that you could speak to King Arthur who is asking for you."

And the former answered him:

"Sir, don't let this weigh upon you. I tell you that I could in no wise go back at this time, and in the name of God don't ascribe it to pride for certainly if I could, I would do it willingly."

"Aha," said the Knight with the Two Swords, "sir, in the name of God, don't say this. If you don't go back you will be causing my death and dishonor, for I have sworn to the king that I would bring you by one means or another."

The knight answered that he would not go back because he could not.

"And know well," said he, "if I went back a misfortune would befall me."

"If you don't go back," said the other, "you will cause me to commit a vile deed because I will attack you with all my strength. It grieves me. God help me because you seem to me to be a worthy man."

"What?" said the other knight. "Shall I have to do battle with you if I don't go back? By my faith I have never heard tell of such madness."

"In the name of God," said the Knight with the Two Swords, "you must come. It grieves me, God help me, but I must follow through, for I have sworn to the king that I would do all in my power to bring you back."

"By my faith," said the other, "I know well that if I come with you some ill fortune will befall me and I shall have to abandon this quest which I have entered upon, and when I have abandoned it, who will take it over?"

"I will take it over," said the Knight with the Two Swords, "and I will never abandon it until I die if I have not achieved it."

"If you will swear it to me," said the knight, "I will go back."
So he swore it to him.

"Now I will go back," said the knight, "but know that I want you to take me into your safe conduct so that any blame will be yours because you have assured me of this."

And he answered that he agreed willingly.

The knight turned around and said to the Knight with the Two Swords:

"Go in front and I will follow."

And so they set out. They went in such a way that they approached the tent, and when they were one bowshot away the knight who was coming behind cried out:

"Ah, sir knight, who carries two swords, I am dead. It was my misfortune to have trusted too much in your protection! I have been killed in your presence and so the shame is yours and the loss mine."

Upon these words the Knight with the Two Swords looked and saw that the other had fallen from his horse onto the ground and he went back and alighted; he found the other knight struck through the body by a spear so powerfully that the steel passed straight through. And he was sadder than anyone could ever be and said:

"Ah, God, I am disgraced since this brave man has died under my protection."

And the knight said to him with great difficulty:

"Sir knight, I am dying. The fault must be yours. Now you must undertake the quest which I had begun and bring it to an end as best you can. Mount on my horse, which is better than yours, and follow the damsel that you saw in my company. She will take you there where you must go and will show you quickly the one who killed me. Then you will see how you can avenge me."

As soon as he said this word he passed away and his soul left his body.

King Arthur arrived before the knight had died and heard a great part of the words that he spoke. The Knight with the Two Swords said to the king:

"Sire, I am dishonored, since this brave man has died under my protection."

"Certainly," said the king, "I have never seen so great a marvel as this, for I saw him struck and I did not see the one who struck him."

Then the knight took the blade with which the other had been struck and pulled it out of his body and said to the king:

"Sire, I am leaving here and I commend you to God's

protection. For I am one who will never enter your court before I have avenged this knight and accomplished the quest which he had begun."

And so he went to the knight's horse, mounted, took his shield, left the camp, and followed the maiden.

The king stayed next to the knight and he was so dumfounded that he didn't know what to say.

As he thus looked at the dead knight, his chamberlain came up to him and said:

"Sire, who has killed this knight?"

"I don't know," said he, "as God is my witness."

Upon these words Merlin appeared among them and said:

"King, don't be so astonished by this happening, for you will see even more amazing ones. Cause a beautiful and rich tomb to be made and put the knight's body in it and have written on it, 'Here lies the Unknown Knight.' And know that on the day you find out his name there will be a joy in your court greater than any you have ever heard of or will ever hear of again. And until that time you will not know."

The king did as Merlin said. Now the tale no longer speaks about the king and Merlin but tells about the Knight with the Two Swords, in order to tell how he achieved the quest, and how he struck the blow through which adventures happened in the realm of Logres, which lasted twenty-two years, and how he and his brother killed each other through mishap.

And know all who wish to hear the tale of my Lord de Boron how he apportioned his book into three parts, all three parts being equal, the first being as long as the second and the second as long as the third. In the first part he breaks off the tale at the beginning of this quest, the second at the beginning of the *Grail*, and the third ends after the death of Lancelot, at which time he tells of the death of King Mark. The present tale he records at the end of the first book so that, should the story of the Grail be corrupted by any adapters after him, all wise men who would apply themselves to listening and hearing them could, through this remark, know whether it was being reported to them wholly or corrupted and would know to what extent things were missing. Having thus outlined the plan of his book, he returns to the tale in the following manner:

Now the tale tells that when the Knight with the Two Swords had left the presence of King Arthur he rode away grieving, sorrowful, and crying, to the place where he had left the maiden. When she saw him coming, she said:

"Ah, sir knight, you have done badly to allow the best knight that I knew in the world to be killed under your safe conduct. Better that you should have died rather than he, and his death will bring you neither renown nor benefit. For just as I was sure that he would finish what he had begun, I now know in truth that you will not have the valor or the strength to accomplish it. You will die a bad and cowardly knight. I truly believe that it would have been much better if death had taken you and left him rather than having things happen the way they did."

The knight was so sad that he didn't know what to say. The damsel left in one direction and the knight in the other. She turned toward the castle and he toward the forest, just as he had planned. When he came to the edge of the forest he met a knight unarmed except for his sword, who had just been hunting and only had two hounds, which were following behind him. The two knights greeted each other when they met, and when the unarmed one saw the Knight with the Two Swords, who was carrying on such great mourning, he stopped in astonishment and thought that it would be bad indeed if he didn't find out the reason for all that sorrow. So he turned right around and said:

"Ah, sir knight, I beg you for God's sake and in the name of chivalry to tell me the cause of all this sadness. For it seems to me that you wouldn't carry on such mourning if it were not for some very serious reason."

"The reason," said the Knight with the Two Swords, "is so serious that I am dishonored forever, and as long as I live I will never be able to gain enough honor to affect the shame which

65

has come to me and for that reason I am mourning this way."

"Oh, my good fellow," said the other, "since this shame is so great that honor cannot stand against it, I beg of you in the name of chivalry and good will that you tell me what the shame was and how it came to you, and I swear to you faithfully as a knight that I will from then on share this shame with you in such a way that I will not abandon you in any situation until that shame be avenged, unless death or your own good will prevents me. And truly I would rather die than that vengeance be not taken."

The Knight with the Two Swords was astonished at what the other offered him because he knew quite well that he had done nothing to deserve such a great favor. Nor would he ever wish to reveal the cause of his mourning because of the evil fate behind it. So he answered even though he was as sad as he was:

"Ah, sir knight, one thing is certain and that is that I will in no wise tell you about it."

"Yes you will, I beg of you, for the love of the one you love most in the world."

"And I tell you," said he, "for the love of the person in the world that I love the most, that I will not tell you at this time. Nor are you as courtly as I thought you were, you who are asking me to tell the truth about myself against my will."

The other knight was deeply grieved and so angered that he thought he was going to lose his mind.

"Certainly you will tell me if I can do anything about it and I would rather die than not know."

So he put out his hand and took hold of the bridle and said to him:

"You're captured, by the Holy Cross. You will not escape me if I have anything to do with it until you have told me what I ask you to."

Then the Knight with the Two Swords abandoned his mourning and began to smile and said:

"By my faith, now I see here the craziest knight that I have ever run across, who thinks he has captured me so easily."

66

And the other held him all the while by the bridle and said to Balain that he was captured. Balain answered that he could escape from this prison when it pleased him. So he put his hand on his sword to frighten the knight, not because he wanted to use it, and said:

"Sir knight, if you don't take your hand off you will be sorry because I will maim you and you will cause me to commit a dastardly deed, because you are unarmed and I am armed."

When the other heard these words he pulled his hand back and said:

"What is this, evil knight? Let God give you a greater shame than you already have. Do you want to strike me thus, unarmed as I am?"

"If I strike you," said the one with the two swords, "it would not be too surprising because you are the most annoying knight, the most vilainous, that I have ever run across, you who want to learn people's secrets by force."

And the other knight answered:

"I have never wanted anything so much as I want this, and since you don't want to say anything of your own free will, I think you will be forced to tell me."

"I don't know what I will do," said the Knight with the Two Swords, "but I don't think you will force me to tell you a thing."

So then the unarmed knight went off along the road in the forest until he came to his dwelling. It had a high and strong tower and sat in the midst of a swamp. And he found his people there who were waiting for him. And he asked them for his arms and they brought them to him and armed him as quickly as they could, but they were not foolhardy enough to ask him where he wanted to go. When they had armed him as he wished, he mounted on his horse, shield on his neck and lance in his hand. And they wanted to follow him, but he quickly forbade it. So he left all alone and rode until he came to the forest and found the tracks. He followed the Knight with the Two Swords and caught up with him at the bottom of the valley. As soon as he saw him he cried out:

"Now I will find out, noble knight, what I asked you before. Now you'll have to do battle."

"What?" said the one with the two swords. "Do I have to fight you or tell you against my will that which I do not want to reveal to any man?"

"For certain," said the other knight, "that is what you have come to. Choose whichever you wish because otherwise you will not be able to leave."

"And I say to you," said he, "that what you are asking me I will not reveal at this time to you nor to anyone else."

"So there's nothing more to do," said the other, "but for you to be on your guard because now you'll have to fight."

And he said that fighting would be better than telling him against his will what he wanted to know.

After this exchange they didn't wait any longer but separated from each other. They were well armed and they were holding their lances in front of them and galloped toward each other and struck in such a way that they hit each other's shields with the steel of their lances. But their mail was so strong and held together so well that they couldn't break as much as one link. The Knight with the Two Swords carried the other knight to the ground so hard that it was a miracle that he didn't break his arms taking such a fall. But he was very hardy and agile and got up quickly and put his hand on his sword and looked as though he wanted to return to the battle. When the other saw this thing he asked him:

"What? Do you want more?"

"Yes," said he. "You will not in any case leave if I can do anything about it. I will indeed know the truth about what I ask of you."

"In truth," said the one with the two swords, "you want to place yourself in risk of death to know something from which you can gain nothing, for when you know it you will gain nothing by it. By my faith, I have never seen such madness."

And the other knight said that in any case he would rather die than not know.

68

So the one with the two swords began to smile and crossed himself out of sheer wonder and said to the other:

"Now mount your horse again, sir knight, and ride with me and I will tell you about my shame. Because it's much better that you know it than that I put myself in a position of killing you or that you should have to kill me, for I think you are an honest man and a good knight."

So the knight thanked Balain warmly for this kindness and quickly mounted and took his lance back, which was still in one piece, and they went off through the forest.

And the one with the two swords began to relate to him the story of the knight whom he had brought back to the tent at King Arthur's request and whom he had undertaken to conduct safely to the king and who was killed under that safe conduct, and he told everything about the way it had happened.

"And because he was killed under my safe conduct and because of evil fate which caused his death, I am mourning and will be very sad for the rest of my life. I will never have joy in my heart until I have avenged him upon the one who killed him. If it is in any way possible to wreak vengeance, I shall not abandon the task, no matter how much pain or effort it costs me. Now I've told you the cause of my sorrow, what I did, and why. Know well that the knight cannot be avenged except by the piece of the very weapon with which he was struck."

"And how will you avenge him," said the other, "without that price?"

"I will certainly have it when I want it," said he, "because a damsel who will accompany me on this quest is carrying it."

"And where is she," said the knight, "if she isn't here with you?"

"She left me just now at the edge of this forest," said the one with the two swords, "and will meet me tomorrow at the cross which is in the middle of the forest."

"Now tell me," said the other knight, "what I'm going to ask you. How do you think you will find the one who caused you this shame when you weren't able to see him when he was standing before you? For if he hadn't been either in front of you or behind you, he couldn't have killed the knight."

"I don't know how he will be found," said the one with the two swords. "But I have undertaken a quest which I will never abandon all the days of my life until I have accomplished it either to my honor or to my shame."

"May Our Lord counsel you," said the other knight, "for certainly here you have a great and grievous task. And because you have told me the truth I will become your companion in the quest. And I make a vow to Our Lord and to all that's good in chivalry that never as long as I live will I abandon it until it is brought to an end either by me or by someone else. And I beg you out of courtesy and chivalry that you help me."

And he said that he would indeed permit it because the other had truly taken on the quest, and so they promised each other to continue to be loyal companions as long as they were together.

So the two knights went along their way. They hadn't gone far before they encountered Merlin, who knew well whatever they had said. He was disguised and was dressed in a robe and hood which were completely white. When he saw the two knights he greeted them and said to them:

"This friendship which you have forged with such difficulty will not last as long as you think because you will be separated quite soon."

"What do you know about it?" said the one with the two swords.

"I am telling you this much now," said Merlin, "and you will not learn anymore about it from me at this time. But now I will reassure you about another thing which you want to know very much. Know truly that the one that you are searching for is the same one who killed the knight in your safe conduct in front of the tent, and he is called Garlan and he is the brother of Pelham."

"I know Pelham well, but I've never known this Garlan. Nevertheless, since I know his name it can't be that I won't find him if ever a man can be found who is looked for."

70

"I advise you," said Merlin, "and counsel you well: turn back and forget about this quest. For truly if you achieve it you will strike a blow from which will come great sorrow and evil to the realm of Logres. The blow of the Vengeful Lance will bring more pain and pestilence than did the blow of a sword which was struck not long ago by King Lambor and King Eurlan. Nor will you have the power to atone for this evil deed, neither you nor any man who now exists. For this entire realm will be afflicted with suffering and destruction and with it many other realms. This desolation will last until he comes who will put an end to all the marvels of Great Britain. You yourself who will be the cause of such terrible sorrow to come, if you go there where you intend to go, will die because of it in great suffering."

"Truly," said the one with the two swords, "even if I must die now a more vile death than any man has ever suffered, I must pursue this quest with all my strength and bring it to an end, whether it mean my death or my life. And even if all the ill fortune in the world should happen because of it, I will not abandon it until I have avenged him who was killed in my safe conduct."

"Now," said Merlin, "you will avenge him, but know that you will repent of it afterward so much that you will wish to be dead rather than alive."

At this the knights left Merlin and continued their way along the high road through the forest as they had been doing before, and Merlin followed along because he wanted to see everything that happened to them.

They went on until they came to a hermitage. In front of this hermitage there was a cemetery, and through the middle of the cemetery passed the road and a path for passers-by. When they had entered the cemetery the Knight with the Two Swords was in front and was thinking very deeply about the words that Merlin had spoken to him, although he did not realize that it had been Merlin. His companion was coming along behind in the best of good spirits. When they were in the midst of the cemetery, the knight who was following let out the cry of a man who had been

71

gravely wounded and said in a loud enough voice so that the one who was in front could hear:

"Ah, sir companion, I am dead. Death has overtaken me because I have stayed so long in your company."

The Knight with the Two Swords was horrified by these words and looked with terror and saw that the knight had fallen from his horse and was lying on the ground as though he were dead. He turned back swiftly, and when he came up to him he climbed down and found that the knight had been struck by a blade full in the body like the other had been, at least as grievously or more so, and the blade was still in one piece. He unlaced his helmet, pulled down his visor, and found that the knight was already dead and that the soul had left the body. He looked all around him and saw nothing born of woman that could have struck this blow. And when he realized that he would not find out then who had done it, he was excessively sad and said:

"Ah, God, what misfortune to not be able to see who has caused me this shame and has done me this great insult this time and the time before."

He began wailing as loud as the other time and said that he was the most unfortunate and the most accursed knight of all those who had ever worn armor, for then he saw clearly that fate was set against him and more inimical to him than toward any other man.

While he was carrying on this way, along came a noble hermit who lived in the hermitage. When he saw such great mourning being carried on by the knight, he began to scold him and blame him quite harshly and said that that was no way for a noble man to act and that it certainly wasn't appropriate for a knight to carry on because of what was happening to him unless it was to repent for his sins; for such a thing, not anything else, should one cry.

"My lord," said the knight, "if I am crying and mourning more than anyone else, there is nothing astonishing about it, because I see that I am more accursed and more unlucky than any man."

And then he told him what had happened to him, with the other knight and with this one.

"Still, my lord," said he, "it would be very consoling to me if I could see the person who killed them so unexpectedly. But this cannot be, it seems, because he seems to be like a phantom. And this is the thing about which I am most sorrowful."

"I say to you," said the good man, "there is no knight errant in the world who doesn't have to face things as they occur, whether they're beautiful or ugly, but truly I greatly marvel at these two things which so suddenly happened to you. Nonetheless, you don't seem to me to be the sort of man who ought to lament about what has befallen him, but rather you seem like one who would take heart and comfort himself. For certainly I don't think that a courageous man would be distressed about adventures which came his way."

Thus spoke the good man to the Knight with the Two Swords. He consoled him a great deal and comforted him more than he had before. The good man had him enter his hermitage and disarm, and then he came back to the knight who was lying dead in the middle of the cemetery and withdrew the blade from the body. And when the good fellow had administered to the body such sacraments as one usually gave to a Christian knight, such as the sacraments of the Holy Church, he put the body in the ground armed as it was, for in those days when they buried a knight they put him in the ground completely armed with his weapons beside him.

When they had buried the knight, they put over the top of him a heavy stone for a tombstone and left him in that way. All day the Knight with the Two Swords stayed with the hermit, who told him many good things and encouraged him strongly to do good deeds.

The next day as soon as the sun had risen and the good man had sung mass, the knight armed himself, mounted his horse, and went to look at the place where lay his companion, whom he could not yet forget. When he arrived there with the hermit, they began to look at the stone with which the spot was covered and found on the top of the stone some carved letters.

The knight asked the man:

"Sir, what do you think of this thing? It doesn't seem to me that all these letters which are engraved here were here last night at all."

"By the grace of God," said the good man, "they weren't. Know you well that this is a miraculous happening. But now look at what they say, for I don't think that they are without great significance."

So the good man began to read the letters and found that they said simply: "In this cemetery Gawain will avenge his father King Lot, for he will cut off the head of King Pellinor during the first ten years after receiving knighthood." The letters formed these words in the way that I have told you. When the one with the two swords heard them, he said:

"Ah, God, what a shame if things happen the way these letters say they will."

"Good sir," said he to the hermit, "do you know about King Pellinor?"

"In truth I do not," said the man.

"Good sir, now know that he is now the best knight I know of in the world and the most noble. For this reason we must curse fortune if he is fated to die thus by the hand of a child that I know will not be worth half of what this knight is worth now. And truly if I weren't on this quest which I've undertaken I would keep him away from that death if I could, because it would be better that I kill Gawain as he is now at this moment than that he kill that noble man, which would be a greater loss than if Gawain were killed."

While they were speaking amongst themselves of this thing, they saw a squire who was coming toward them at a great speed. He greeted them straightaway on behalf of Merlin and said to them:

"Merlin tells you that he carved these letters last night and don't be astonished by what they say because things will happen just as you see them written."

"Truly," said the one with the two swords, "it is a great shame. We would indeed suffer a much lesser loss by the death of Gawain than by Pellinor's."

"That is not the case," said the squire. "Merlin commanded me to tell you that Gawain will be a better knight when he reaches his mature age than is King Pellinor. And for that reason you should not be sorrier about the death of one than the other."

As the squire finished speaking he left them and went away at a gallop. The Knight with the Two Swords, as soon as he had lost sight of the squire, said to the good man who was with him:

"Sir, I cannot stay here any longer. I commend you to God and for the sake of God remember me in your prayers and supplications."

The hermit told him he would not forget and stayed in the cemetery.

The knight went back to the forest and rode toward the place where he thought he would find the damsel. When he arrived at the cross he found that she was there already, down off her horse to rest, and was sitting in front of the cross waiting for him to come. They greeted each other as soon as they saw each other, and she said to him:

"Sir knight, you've taken a lot longer than you should have. Have you discovered anything which is of use to you?"

"Damsel," said he, "yes. Since I left you something has happened to me about which I am very sad and very angry and that's why I have been delayed."

He told her straightaway the truth about the knight he had taken into his safe conduct whom someone had killed at his side so suddenly that he couldn't tell who did it. When she heard about this thing she began to sigh and said:

"Ah, alas, that was the way in which my friend was killed, the most courtly, the best knight that I knew in the world."

"Damsel," said the knight, "things are so. One must accept what happens, however it comes about in this world."

"These adventures," she said, "which cause good men to die because of so evil a fate are more shameful and unfortunate than others."

"Mount," he said, "because we must not tarry."

75

She mounted straightaway and they went on through the forest and rode thus until the hour of vespers.

At the hour of vespers it happened that they came to a castle in a valley which appeared to be very fine in every way and which was surrounded by walls and moats. The knight rode ahead and the damsel followed far behind. As soon as he got inside the castle those who were up on the wall let a portcullis fall so that the knight was inside and the damsel was outside. When he saw that he was shut in and that the damsel remained outside, he didn't know what he could do because he couldn't go back, nor could she come forward. While he was considering what to do, he listened and heard the damsel who had remained outside begin to shout:

"Oh, Knight with the Two Swords who has left me outside, help me or I am dead! For there in the castle is the woman who hates me the most in the world; who wants to have my head cut off even though I don't deserve it. If you tarry too long I will be killed before you come."

When he heard the damsel he was so distressed that no one could be more so, for he couldn't get out of there in any way unless he climbed over the wall, and if she died while in his company he would never regain his honor. So he got down off his horse and went to the door of the tower, found it open, and went inside. He climbed up as fast as he could, and when he stepped onto the top he found as many as a dozen soldiers guarding the tower, but they were at that moment completely unarmed. He took his sword in his hand and shouted to them saying that they were all dead if they didn't open the gate. When they saw him all dressed in armor coming toward them with sword drawn, they were afraid of him and they didn't wait for him to strike because they were unarmed, so they fled one in this direction and another in that. When he came to the window of the tower to look outside to see why the damsel was shouting, he put his head out and saw the damsel with two knights. One knight was saying to the lady who had come with Balain:

76

"If you don't do what we require of you, you cannot get away without being killed : we will cut your head off straightaway. And know that what we require of you is the custom of the castle and no damsel comes here who does not comply with it."

And she, who saw she was trapped, and who was afraid of dying, asked what it was that they wanted of her.

"We will tell you," they said, "when you have sworn to us that you will do it. And know that it is nothing that will dishonor you."

She swore straightaway because she didn't think help would come from any source. The Knight with the Two Swords, who saw that they were pressing her hard, was so distressed that no one could be more so. He couldn't get to her in any way without jumping down from the tower, since he could not open the door, neither a crack nor wide. So he said to himself, it is better to die if die he must than to have the damsel die because of his failure to act. So he crossed himself and commended himself to Our Lord and jumped straightaway down off the tower. However, he was fortunate enough that he escaped unhurt and so he climbed up out of the moat, and when he came up to the damsel he put his hand on his sword and said to those who were with her that they had done an evil thing to lay hands on her. The two who had seen the jump that he had made were all amazed by the marvel which they were witnessing, so they let the damsel go and drew back for fear of the one with the two swords. He came up to the damsel, took her by the hand, and said to her:

"My young lady, why were you shouting just now ?"

"Sir," she said, "because they wanted to kill me if I didn't swear to them to keep the custom of the castle. And they were pressing me so hard that I swore it to them so that I would not be shamed."

"It grieves me," said he, "that they got your promise, because I fear that they're going to hold you to it, but I don't know what I can do for a horse because I left mine inside."

So while he was speaking about this thing to the damsel, he looked and saw the gate open which just now had been closed,

77

and there came out of it as many as ten knights all armed, leading his horse. They gave it back to the knight and said to him:

"Here you are, sir knight, for we don't want to keep anything that belongs to you."

And he was very happy about this, so he took it and then they said to the damsel:

"Damsel, acquit yourself now of your promise. You ought to do it because to do otherwise would be dishonesty and perjury."

"Truly," said she, "I am ready if it is something that I can do."

Now came among them another damsel and she was carrying in her hand a fairly large silver bowl, and when she saw the damsel she said to her:

"Damsel, you must fill this bowl for us with your blood; such is the custom of this castle. Otherwise no damsel who comes here may pass by. And if you don't do it we will know that you have proven yourself to be dishonest, and if you do it gracefully we shall look upon it as a noble gesture, and if you don't do it of your own free will, then you will do it under constraint, because no foreign damsel may leave here without doing it."

When the damsel understood that which she was being asked to do, she was terrified and didn't know how to answer, so she said:

"I would truly like to know, before I place myself in danger of death, why you need such a great river of my blood, for if some noble thing can come of it I will not refuse, but if neither good nor ill can come of it I will in no way undergo such suffering because it would lead to my death, I think."

The maid answered her:

"I'll tell you what it's about. Then I think you'll do it more cheerfully. In truth, the lady of this house has recently contracted a malady which is as ugly and as horrible as leprosy, and she is so severely afflicted by it that you've never seen a lady more seriously ill than she. We are very worried and anxious that she be cured if possible, but that hasn't yet been the will of Our Lord. We have sought a great deal of advice, from near and far, and we have only found one old and venerable man who could give us advice and

78

who said to us: 'I will tell you how she can be cured if you want to do it.' We told him that we would do it if it wasn't too burdensome a thing. He continued and told us: 'If you are willing to arrange to get from a maid, virgin in spirit and deed, daughter of a king and queen, a full bowl of blood and rub it on your lady, her illness will be cured.' Thus the good man showed us how to effect the lady's cure. We swore thereupon that no damsel would pass by here who didn't conform to that plan. Therefore by rights you must accede to it as the others before you have done."

The maiden answered then:

"You certainly have here," said she, "a most unappealing and ugly custom, but because the other girls who passed by observed it, I will too even if I die on the spot. I think that it is more probable that I'll die of it than be well, for there isn't a girl in the world strong enough to survive it if she lost as much blood as this dish would hold."

The Knight with the Two Swords stepped briskly forward and spoke so loudly that everyone could hear and understand him clearly:

"Young lady, I forbid you to do it, for be assured that you cannot escape death if you do it, and if you die now in this way, who would lead me on this quest that I have undertaken, which I cannot accomplish without your aid?"

"My heart tells me," said she, "that I will not die from it, and that's why I'm doing it with greater confidence."

He was very angry, but didn't dare stop her.

They led the maid into the castle and the knight as well. When they came to the donjon they disarmed the knight. Although he didn't want to stay there (for the damsel asked him to stay the night) in order to see what end she came to, he said he would remain the night, and only because he was worried about her.

Then there arrived six maidens who uncovered her arms and said that they would take as much blood as they had to. They caused her blood to spurt forth from both arms and took as much as they wanted. The maiden fainted because of the blood she had lost, and they stanched the flow and carried her into one of the rooms to rest.

The Knight with the Two Swords was very worried about the girl all night and was very much afraid that she would die, for he didn't see how he could accomplish his quest since he didn't know where to search for the one who had killed the knight in front of the tent. He had already learned this much: that it was a knight who had the power to hide himself so that no one could see him as he was wandering about if he didn't want to be seen. But when he was not wandering, he could not make himself invisible.

The knight thought about the maiden a great deal all through the night, because he was very much afraid that she would die. The next day, as soon as the sun was up, before he had heard mass and taken up his arms, he went into the room where she lay, straight to her bed, greeted her and asked her how she was and how she felt. She returned his greeting and told him that she felt no pain, thanks to God, and that she could ride now.

"But how is the lady of the house? Is she cured?"

"Certainly not," said he, "she is still not cured."

"May God be pleased," said she, "that she not recover nor be cured of her malady, but that Death take her soon, and that would certainly be a great joy. Let no one, for the sake of a woman's illness, ever more be subjected to such an evil and treacherous custom as they have here! For certainly, in my opinion, a thousand damsels more will die from it who have not deserved it."

"Damsel," said the knight, "get ready, for we must not stay here longer, dress and we will ride away."

"I want to get out of here," said she, "never has any household treated me so ill."

Thereupon the knight went to don his armor. And the people there said to him:

"Sir, will you not hear mass here before you leave?"

"I will not," said he, "for the situation here has so distressed me that I am sorry I ever came in."

Then the knight and the damsel, who was already dressed,

mounted, but she was thin and pale because of the blood she had lost. When they had mounted they left the castle and commended to the Devil all those within, and they went out and went away.

Thus the damsel had followed the custom of the castle and escaped and did not die because of it: and she was better off than the others who came after her because none came there without dying from it. This horrible custom continued for a very long time, and the lady of the castle did not die nor was she cured until that valiant maid, the sister of Perceval of Wales, came there and resolved the adventure of the castle. The lady was cured by her blood as soon as she was rubbed with it, as will be plainly told in the *Great Quest of the Grail*. But now the tale no longer tells about it, for I will indeed tell the truth of the matter when the time is right.

Now the tale tells that the Knight with the Two Swords rode with the maiden all day, the next day, the third day, and the fourth, without encountering any adventure which was worthy of mentioning in the account. They rode together in this way day after day so that they were very far from the city of Camelot, and the language began to change so much that they could understand little.

One night they were lodged at the edge of a wood in the home of a very fine gentleman who offered them the best fare and most cordial welcome that he could. When the table had been set and they were seated there, the knight listened and heard, in one of the nearby rooms, the voice of a man moaning in anguish. This wailing lasted the whole time they were at table. He would have liked to ask what it was, but he didn't dare question his host as long as they were sitting at table. After the meal when the tables had been cleared, the knight said to his host:

"Kind host, if I did not think it might offend you, I would ask you something that I would very much like to know."

"Speak," said the good man, "and I will tell it to you if it is something that I know."

"I ask you," said he, "to tell me who it is that is moaning in one of the rooms in this house."

"Certainly, fair guest," said the good man, "I will willingly tell you that. Know that it is a son of mine who is in much pain and agony from a wound which he has recently received. It happened so suddenly that he didn't see who it was that wounded him. It was near the hour of noon and when he was wounded he was surrounded by no walls nor trees which could have prevented him from seeing the one who did it. For that reason I think it was some kind of enchantment."

To this the Knight with the Two Swords answered, saying:

"Host, I tell you that it was not a spell, but a knight who has the power to remain unseen when he wishes as long as he is mounted. Know, host, that even though he has struck your son in the way you describe, he has done something to me which is worse: he killed a knight who was in my safe conduct, about which I am so sad that it weighs upon me more heavily than if he had mortally wounded me."

And then he told him about the knight whom he had sent back to the tent out of devotion to King Arthur:

"...and he killed him while he was in my safe conduct," and about the other knight whom he had recently accepted as companion on the quest:

"...who was also killed behind my back in a similar manner."

Then the host began to cross himself with amazement.

"Good host," said the one with the two swords, "do you know this knight's name?"

"Indeed I do not," said the host, "for I have never heard tell of him."

"Now know this, good host, that his name is Garlan and he is the brother of King Pelham, the King of Listinois."[9]

The host crossed himself and said:

"By my head, I believe what you're telling me. I know this Garlan well, and it wasn't a year ago that he said something to me, which I remember well, which shows that he struck my son so that he now is wounded. It happened that he and I went to a tourna-

9. Merlin had told Balain his name earlier on (cf. p. 70).

ment, and it happened that I unhorsed him twice that day, in front of everyone there. And when he, who was much richer than I, saw that he couldn't get the better of me, he told me that he would make me grieve for the person I held dearest before the year was out. He has certainly kept his word, I think, because he has mortally wounded my son, the man I loved most in the world."

"O God," said the one with the two swords, "how can I find him? There is no man in the world I would more like to see than him."

"In truth," said the host, "I will tell you how you can find him and see him face to face if you do what I instruct you to."

The knight answered that he would spare no effort until he had done it.

"Now I will tell you how you will achieve it," said the host. "It is true that King Pelham of Listinois will hold great and sumptuous court a week from Sunday at the Castle of the Perilous Palace. Garlan will serve at this feast; I know truly that he will. And gentlemen from many realms will be with him. If you can get in there on that day, know that you will find him."

When the one with the two swords heard this news he was happier than he had been before and answered:

"Gentle host, God be blessed that he brought me to this place. Now I know that this thing you have told me and instructed me in will indeed bring my quest to an end if ever it is to be."

And then he said to the damsel and to his host again:

"Fair host, do you think that your son can be cured?"

"In truth," said he, "I don't know what to say, for he is very seriously wounded. Nevertheless, an old man who stayed here a week ago told me that my son would be cured, but that it would not happen before his wound had been rubbed with the blood of the knight that wounded him. And I asked him who had told him this and he told me, 'Merlin the wizard told me to tell you this and that he could not be cured otherwise.'"

Upon hearing these words, the Knight with the Two Swords said:

"Good host, if it is thus that your son must be cured by the blood of that man, know that he will be cured, if you or someone else of your household wants to come with me. If it happens thus that I can find him, no blood of man has ever been as amply shed as will be the blood of this one in whatever place I may find him, even if I have to die on the spot."

"And I swear to you," said the host, "that I will follow you to that place, because there is nothing that I want as much as I do my son's good health. Moreover, I promise you that I will put you on the shortest road."

And he thanked him very much for it.

That night the Knight with the Two Swords was very much at ease, very well lodged, and was very happy about the news that he had heard there. In the morning as soon as the day had broken, he got up and heard mass in the house, where there was a small chapel. Afterward he armed himself and mounted and started off on the road with the damsel and his host. Thus they rode together a whole week and the next without encountering any adventure worthy of the telling, until they all finally arrived at the castle where King Pelham was holding court, and they entered, all three of them, at the hour of prime. The feast was arranged in such a way that no knight could come into the court if he didn't bring with him his sister or his lady. If he came some other way he could by no means enter. The Knight with the Two Swords and the damsel entered, and the host remained outside because he had no lady with him and he was much grieved by this.

As soon as they had gone inside they found so great a company of knights that it seemed that all the knights of the realm of Logres had been assembled there. When the host's men saw him armed they ran up to meet him and had him get down from the horse, and they took him to one of the rooms and his lady with him.[10] They quickly disarmed him and brought him a clean tunic to put on so that he would be presentable; they had plenty of clothing there. They took him into the palace to sit down with the other

10. The lady with Balain was his host's daughter.

knights, but no one could take the sword which he had on from him. He said that it was a custom of his country that no knight would eat in a strange place, even in such a high place as in the king's court, without having his sword on, and if they didn't want to allow him to follow the custom of his country he would leave the way he had come. So they allowed him to do it. Many were the knights that King Pelham had assembled there and when the hour to dine came, the tables were set and they all sat down except the ones who were to serve. The feast was arranged in such a way that each knight had his lady next to him. So they started to serve many beautiful and rich things. The Knight with the Two Swords began to ask a knight who was sitting to his left:

"Tell me, which one is Garlan, the brother of King Pelham?"

And he showed him to him and said:

"See him there, the tall one, the knight with the red hair, the most amazing knight in the world."

"Why is he amazing?" said the one with the two swords, as though he didn't know. He asked this so that he would better know the truth.

"Because," said the other knight, "when he is armed nobody from whom he ever wishes to hide himself can see him." [11]

"By my faith," said he, "you tell me marvels. I really can't believe that it's true."

"Yes, it is true," said the other knight.

"Now tell me," said the one with the two swords, "if he had wronged you so that he deserved death, how would you avenge yourself, because he would elude you as soon as he was armed."

"By my faith," said the other, "if he had done me ill I would take him wherever I found him, armed or unarmed."

"You could only find him if he were unarmed, as you yourself have told me."

"And unarmed I would capture him," said the other.

11. At various places in the text, different reasons for Garlan's invisibility are given: his wandering (p. 80), his being mounted (p. 82), or his being armed (p. 85). The remanieur does not resolve the contradiction in the text.

85

"True, but if you are armed and he is unarmed, and you lay a hand on him, then everyone would call you dishonorable and cowardly."

"By no means," said he, "if it were a question of vengeance. I have told you what I would do, and no one could do any other."

So then the Knight with the Two Swords began to think, and when he had thought for quite a bit he looked at the one who had killed the knight in his safe conduct and was so enraged that no one could be more so. For if he escaped him this time, he thought he would never see him again. If he killed him now in front of King Pelham and the entire assembly he didn't see how he could escape from there without being killed and dismembered, even if he had the strength of six of the best knights in the world. He didn't know what to do about this, nor what course to follow. For if he killed him here and now he could not escape death and if Garlan escaped him he thought he would never find him again. These two things preoccupied him greatly and he was in such distress that he neither drank nor ate, but kept on thinking. These thoughts lasted until all the dishes had arrived on the table and he could have got up then in the same condition as he sat down in, for he had neither eaten nor drunk. Garlan, the red-haired knight, who was going around amongst the tables serving, noticed this thing and saw clearly that he had neither drunk nor eaten, and he took it as a very great insult because he thought that the knight was leaving his food and drink out of scorn. Then Garlan went up to Balain and raised his hand and gave him a great blow in the face so that it turned red and said to him:

"Raise your head, sir knight, and eat like the others as the seneschal commands you. And cursed be he who taught you to sit at a noble man's table when you are doing nothing but thinking."

When the Knight with the Two Swords saw that he had been struck in such a way he was so angry that he lost his senses and control and answered:

"Garlan, this is not the first pain that you have caused me."

And Garlan aswered:

"So avenge yourself if you can."

"I will," said the one with the two swords, "sooner than you dare think."

He put his hand on his sword and said:

"Garlan, you see before you the knight that you have caused to follow you from King Arthur's court with great difficulty and travail. Never will an honest man strike a man at a king's table nor kill a knight treacherously."

Then he struck him with his sword on the head so hard that he split it as far as his chest knocking him to the ground and then he shouted:

"Host, you may now take the blood of Garlan to cure your son."

Then he said to the damsel:

"Damsel, bring me the piece of the weapon with which the knight was struck in front of the tents."

And she brought to him the fragment of the weapon which she had with her. And he took it and jumped away from the table and struck Garlan who was lying dead on the floor with it so hard that it pierced him from one side to the other, and then he said loud enough so that everyone could hear him:

"Now it doesn't matter what is done with me because I have completed my quest."

Thereupon a great hubbub arose in the court and they all shouted:

"Seize him, seize him!"

The king, who was beside himself because his brother had been killed in his presence, shouted:

"Seize that man for me, but be careful not to kill him."

The one with the two swords answered:

"Sir king, don't command that I be seized but come forward yourself! You have to do it, I think, because you are considered one of the best knights in the world."

The king was without doubt a very fine knight and very faithful to God. Nor did anyone know in all of Britain at that time any prince who was as much loved by Our Lord. He was over-

taken with wrath and anger both because of the death of his brother
and because of the words of the knight, so he said that indeed he
would avenge him if he could, and so he got up from the table and
said to all the others:

"Be careful that none of you be so foolhardy as to put a hand
upon him, because I intend to overcome him by myself."

Then he ran and seized a great wooden pole which was in the
room, took a hold of it, lifted it up, and ran toward the one who
held the drawn sword, not the sword with which he killed the
damsel, but another.[12] When the Knight with the Two Swords
saw him coming he didn't retreat but held up his sword, and the
king assailed him with a cross stroke and struck the sword so hard
that he broke it just above the hilt so that the blade fell on the floor
and the hilt[13] stayed in his hand. When the one with the two
swords saw what happened, he was greatly afraid, so he rushed
into another room because he thought he might find some weapon there. But when he got there he didn't find anything of the
sort, so he was more afraid than before because he saw that the
king was following him brandishing the pole. Then he sprang into
another room even farther on, but he didn't find any more there
than in the other one except that he saw that the rooms were the
most beautiful in the world and the richest that anyone had ever
seen. He looked and saw that the door of a third room was open
which was even farther on and so he headed in that direction to

12. On page 9 Balain beheaded the supposed "Lady of the Lake" with the
Sword with the Strange Hangings which he wrested from the damsel who had
brought it from the Lady of the Isle of Avalon. Since then he has not used
it and won't until he fights his brother at the end of the tale (p. 111 ff.). Since he
breaks his second sword here, he has to go rushing through the palace looking
for a weapon. If this is true where was the other sword and why didn't he use
it? For a complete discussion of this unresolved dilemma see Eugène Vinaver,
The Rise of Romance, (New York: Oxford University Press, 1971), chap. IV,
"The Waste Land."

13. This is where the Huth MS breaks off. The missing text, which is sup-
plied from the Cambridge MS, ends with the words: "...and gave him to
Merlin," on p. 93.

enter it, for he still thought he might find some arms there with which he could defend himself against the one who was following right behind him. And when he entered there he heard a loud voice which said to him:

"Woe betide you who have entered here for you are not worthy of entering such a holy place."

He heard the voice clearly but didn't stop for all of that, but went on into the room and found that it was so beautiful and rich that he thought that there was not in all the world one of equal beauty. The room was square and marvelously large and smelled good, as though all the spices of the world had been brought there. In one place in the room there was a very large and reasonably high silver table which sat on three silver pillars. On the table, right in the middle, was a vessel of silver and gold, and in this vessel was a lance standing up, the point pointing downward and the shaft pointing up. And whoever looked at the lance closely would wonder how it stood straight because it was not supported on either one side or the other. The Knight with the Two Swords looked at the lance but didn't realize what it was so he went toward it and heard another booming voice which thundered:

"Don't touch it, sinner."

But he didn't hesitate because of these words and he took the lance in his two hands and struck King Pelham, who was already behind him, so hard that he pierced both of his thighs, and the king fell to the ground because he was very severely wounded. And the knight pulled back the lance to him and put it back in the vessel where he'd taken it from, and as soon as he had put it back it stood as straight as it had before.

When he had done this, he turned back quickly toward the hall, since it seemed to him that he had been well avenged. But before he got there the whole palace began to tremble and so did all the rooms within, and all the walls shook so hard that it seemed that they were about to tip over and fall apart. And all those who were in the palace were so frightened by this marvel that there was no one who was strong enough to remain standing, and they began to fall, one here and one there as though they were dead. They all had their eyes closed because they were expecting right then and there that they would all fall into the abyss. And because they saw that the palace was shaking and trembling so hard that it must very soon fall down, they thought that the end of the world had indeed come and that they would have to die now.

Then sounded among them a voice, blasting like a trumpet which said clearly:

"Now begin the adventures and marvels of the Adventurous Realm which will not cease until the handling of the Holiest Lance by profane and sullied hands which have wounded the most worthy of princes has been dearly paid for. So, because of this, the High Master will take his vengeance on those who have not deserved it."

And this voice was heard by all the castle, and everyone was so afraid because of it that they fainted. And the true tale tells that they lay in a swoon two nights and two days. From this great fear more than a hundred of them died in the palace. Of the others who were within the walls but not in the palace, many died from fear and others were wounded and maimed because several houses of the city fell, and a great part of the wall fell because of the shock which the castle made, and so were knights and commoners wounded in this way. And of all these there were some who were not in any way wounded, but certainly there was no one brave enough in all the city to dare enter the palace in the first two days, nor would anyone have entered there if it hadn't been for Merlin, who came to see the great tragedy which had come to pass there, both to the rich and to the poor, for he knew well that a blow could not be struck with the Vengeful Lance without bringing on some miraculous event. When he came to the castle, he found them so wounded and in such bad condition that the fathers could not aid the sons nor the sons the fathers. Of those who were the healthiest, no one was hardy enough to dare enter the palace because they thought that everyone in it was dead. When Merlin came he asked them what happened to the fortress, and they all said with one voice:

"Sire, we know nothing of it. We have not gone there because we think that there is no one in the palace who has not come to harm."

"Aha," said he, "you are the most miserable people and the most cowardly that I have ever seen, you who don't dare go there to see how King Pelham, your lord, is or whether he is dead or alive. Follow me. I will go first and we will see how he is."

"Go," they said, "and we will follow you."

Then Merlin came to the gate of the palace and entered and found at the gateway a porter and two guards who were lying dead, since they were among those who had been crushed by a section of the tower wall which had fallen on them.

"These three," said Merlin, "you can take them and put them in the ground because they no longer have need of a doctor because they have been dead more than one day."

They took them. Merlin went on and found in the court a full two hundred knights and guards lying on the ground, some dead from fright and others from stones or planks that had fallen on them. Some others were lying not dead but they were as though in a swoon, for they thought that the miracle they had witnessed was going to last forever. Those who were alive Merlin raised up and comforted them a great deal and said to them:

"Get up for you're in no danger. The tempest you were so afraid of is over."

And they answered:

"Sire, do you speak the truth?"

"Yes," said he, "be quite reassured."

Then those who could got up and those who didn't have the strength to raise themselves were carried into the town to get well and rest. So Merlin went into the great palace. When he got up there he found lying in the great hall more than 700 knights, damsels, and squires, many of them dead, and most of them didn't have the strength to sit up, so they were as though dead. Merlin spoke to them loud enough so that they could all hear:

"Those of you who are alive get up! The thing that has terror-
ized you so is over."

When they heard these words, they sat up and opened their eyes
like people coming out of a dream and asked:

"Ah! God, is the storm over?"

"Yes," said Merlin, "get up and be reassured."

Then those who could got up; those who couldn't were carried
to various places. Merlin went along from room to room and soon
he came near the chamber where the Holy Lance was and the
Holy Vessel that they called the Grail. He quickly knelt down
and said to those who were near him:

"Ah, God! What a thing he has brazenly done, the wretched,
sinful, ill-fated one who, with his sullied and profane hands,
expelled from the garden because of his evil and poisoned by
debauch, touched so sacred and precious a shaft as I see there, and
with it wounded so noble a man as King Pelham! Ah, God! How
dearly will be ransomed such a great outrage and misdeed; how
dearly will pay for it those who didn't deserve it; how much will
the noble gentlemen and good knights of the realm of Logres
endure pain and trial because of it, and how many miracles and
perilous adventures will occur because of that Dolorous Stroke
that was struck!"

Thus spoke Merlin, while weeping bitterly both in his heart and
from his eyes. When he had said his prayers and devotions at the
door of the chamber as well as he knew them, he stood up and
asked those who were near him:

"Is there no priest in your company?"

"Yes," they said, "a White Monk."

Merlin called him and said to him:

"Sir, if you have the arms of Jesus Christ, put them on."

"I do not have them," said he, "but I know well that they are in
one of the chambers here, because I myself put them there the day
the great tragedy struck this castle."

"Sir," said Merlin, "go get them and put them on and go into this room, for otherwise no one can enter this holiest of places unless he is wearing the sign of Jesus Christ."

The good man thought that Merlin was telling him the truth, so he did what he told him. When he was all dressed as though he was about to say mass, Merlin said to him:

"Sir, now you can enter safely, for you are well armed to enter a most holy place. Enter, and bring out to me the knight that you find there and King Pelham and put them outside so that we can carry them where we will."

And he did just as Merlin asked him and he brought out the knight who still lay in a swoon and gave him to Merlin.[14] Merlin called him by his true name and said:

"Balain, open your eyes."

And he said:

"Ah, God, where am I?"

"You are still," said Merlin, "at King Pelham's palace where you have acted in such a way that from now on everyone in the whole world who knows you will hate you and wish you ill."

The knight did not answer anything that Merlin said because he felt that he was indeed guilty of what Merlin had accused him of, but he asked him how he could leave there since, as he had said, he had finished his quest.

Merlin said:

"Follow me and I will take you out of this castle, because if those in this castle recognized you and knew that the evil which they have suffered is because of you, no man would prevent them from cutting you in pieces before you got to the gate."

"Have you any news of the damsel who came here with me?" asked the knight.

"Indeed, in truth," said Merlin, "you can see her dead in the midst of this palace. She has so much profited from accompanying you that you have caused her to be killed."

The knight was very sad about the news that Merlin told him, but he saw that whatever Merlin told him was indeed the truth,

14. See n. 13, p. 88.

and he asked Merlin to lead him out of there because he had no reason to remain now that the damsel was dead.[15]

"Truly," said Merlin, "even if you hadn't asked me, I would have done it, because I don't want you to be dead yet."

So the knight got up off the ground where he was still lying and Merlin led him out of the palace. When they came into the courtyard they found many people wounded, crippled, and dead, and Merlin said to the knight:

"All of this ravage you have caused here. Now see what you have done."

"It is so," said the knight, "since it is done. It cannot be undone."

"That is true," said Merlin.

So they went down away from the city until they came to the gates and passed outside. The knight was equipped with his shield and his lance and all of his armor, of which he had left nothing inside except for his sword which he had lost, as the tale has already told.

Merlin said to him:

"You've lost your horse."

"It's true," said the knight, "I don't know what happened to it, so I'll have to go on foot, I think."

"You will not," said Merlin, "if I can help it. Wait for me here and I'll come back right away."

So Merlin went to the castle and managed to find a good and strong horse and brought it to the knight, for he found no man who stood in his way. And he gave it to the knight and he mounted. Then Merlin said to him:

"Do you know why I am doing this good deed for you? Know that it is not for you as much as it is for love of King Arthur, whose knight you are. I know it well."

---

15. "The damsel" referred to here is the one who had come to the castle with Balain and who had long ago set out to accompany him on his quest. The collapsing castle killed her.

And the knight answered:

"You have indeed done me a great good service. I would like, if it pleases you, to know who you are?"

"I will tell you," said Merlin. "I am Merlin the Wizard, he about whom so many people speak. I don't know whether you have ever heard speak of me."

And then the knight did obeisance and said:

"Merlin, I didn't know you. Neither do they who are more acquainted with you. I may or may not ever see you again as chance dictates, but whether I see you again or not, know that I am your knight in whatever place I might be, and I should indeed be, because you have been of more help to me than any man has ever been."

"I know," said Merlin, "what you would do for me, if I required it of you. Go with God. May God lead you and protect you from accursed fate wherever you go."

So they took leave of each other and Merlin went off into the castle, and the knight as he was going away from the city found outside the walls his host dead from a piece of the battlement which had fallen upon him. And so he was very sad because then he knew better the extent of his ill deed than he had before. After he had looked around for quite a while he went on his way. As he rode through the countryside, he found the trees bent and broken and the crops destroyed and everything as wasted as though lightning had struck everywhere, and indeed it did strike in many places, but not everywhere. He found in the cities half of the people dead, both city dwellers and knights. In the fields he found the farm people dead. What can I tell you? He found everything in the realm of Listinois destroyed, so that it was from then on called by everyone the realm of the Waste Land and the Realm of the Outcast Land because the land was so strange and so wasted throughout. And as he passed through the cities, all those who saw him, were they good or evil, said to him:

"O knight, you have condemned us all to poverty and desolation from which we don't ever expect to escape. Let God take you some place where you will be massacred by fierce weapons, because you have done us so much ill that the entire world could not repair it, and we will not avenge ourselves upon you, but God, who is the sovereign avenger, will avenge us, and He will see that you are involved in an ill-fated adventure which will make us very happy and joyous when we find out about it."

Thus spoke the great and the small in all the cities where he went, and he was so sad about it and so angry that he wanted the lightning from the sky to come down upon him and destroy him because he knew indeed that he had done such an evil thing that he could never hope to see God nor could he ever again be in as good a position as he was before. Thus he rode for five whole days and he found no land which was not wasted and given over to pain and destruction. He slept each evening in mountains where he found ancient and deep forests, and every hermit who received him in his dwelling said to him:

"Sir, we will not shelter you except for the love of God and the honor of chivalry, for you have put us in a state of poverty and woe which we have not deserved and from which we will never recover through you."

And when the good men said such things to the knight he didn't know how to answer them because he knew well that they spoke the truth, and he was so unhappy that no one could be more so. And thus he rode day after day because he wanted very much to get out of this land where he had done such a thing. And when it pleased God he was out of it and he came back to beautiful country and he was fairly well comforted, more than he was before, and he rode on this way for eight days wherever his way led him without finding any adventure worth the telling.

On the ninth day it happened that chance brought him to a great and deep forest and he entered and rode along a path all alone without company. He wandered in this way from the morning until the hour of noon. At that hour it happened that he came into a great valley in front of a tower and found there a tall stud tethered to a tree. He stopped to see whose horse it was, for he

thought that it could not be without a master, and he began to
look all around him. While he was looking around he saw, at the
foot of the tower, a tall knight who was well built in every way, a
man of such fine appearance in every way that I don't think that I
could tell you of any more handsome a one. He was seated on the
ground on the green grass and thinking so intently that no one
could be more pensive. The Knight with the Two Swords looked
at the one who was thinking so intently and was amazed that this
could be. And so he stood thus thinking quite a while. After quite
a while, the knight heaved a great sigh, then said:

"My joy is so long from me!"

Then the one with the two swords thought that if this knight
keeps thinking for a long time, since he is all alone, and the one he's
waiting for does not come, he could get himself into a bad
situation because enemies readily attack people who are without
company. So he stepped forward and softly said to the knight:

"God save you, sir knight, and send you joy, for it seems to me
that you have need of it."

He came to himself right away but he was so angry that someone had snatched him from his thoughts that no one could be
more pained, and he answered in great anger:

"Get away from here, sir! You who have snatched away my
thoughts have killed me. I don't think that I have ever been as
content as I was just now. Cursed be the hour that you came here."

Then he began to think again as intently as he had before. And
when the Knight with the Two Swords saw this, he backed away
and he was very sorry that he had spoken to him because he had
caused him such great annoyance, he was sure of that. And when
he had retreated a bit, he stopped because he wanted to see, if he
could, what would come of this thinking in which the other was
so earnestly engaged. So he waited there until the hour of none to
see if the other would come out of his thought, but he did not
even move, he just kept on thinking. Around the hour of none he
heaved a great sigh, even greater than before, and said:

"Oh, my lady, you who are so late in coming have assured my

97

death. If you wait any longer you will never see me again other than dead."

Then he was quiet and said nothing more, and the one with the two swords knew that it was of some lady or damsel that the knight was thinking so intently and he was very sorry for it. Because of this he would not leave here all day long. He would wait in this way until night to see if she for whom this knight was in such great pain would come.

After the hour of vespers when the sun had already begun to set, the knight said:

"Ah, lady, you will cause me to die by your deeds and by your requirements. I cannot wait any longer."

So then he drew his sword from the scabbard and said:

"Lady, you gave me my death when you gave me this sword. I will now die because of it, since I can't stand this great pain any longer in which I am plunged night and day on account of you."

When the one with the two swords saw this thing he got up from beneath the tree where he had been seated for a long time and saw that he had best not hesitate for he knew that the other would kill himself now if the sword weren't taken out of his hands. So he jumped forward and grabbed him by the hand with which he was holding the sword and said:

"Ah, sir knight, for the sake of God have mercy on yourself. What is it that you want to do? Do you want to destroy your body and lose your soul?"

The other one looked at him thereupon and was so unhappy at not having done what he intended that he thought that it were better if he were dead and said then:

"If you don't let me have my sword of your own free will, I'll have it in spite of you. I will kill you first and myself afterward. And then the tragedy will be all the greater because it will not concern me alone. Therefore I beg of you to leave it to me."

"I will let you keep it if you agree," said the one with the two swords, "to tell first who you are and who is the one whom you love so much. I swear as a knight that if you are willing to tell me thus what I ask about you that I will never sleep until I have brought back to you the one that you are so unhappy about, if it can be done by travail and effort that one might put into it. Know that I do nothing so willingly or with so much good will as I will do this thing to put you at your ease, for I have never seen a knight as unhappy as you were when I found you."

When the other heard these words he restrained himself a great deal from being hostile and said:

"Who are you who are offering me such a wonderful thing? I beg you that you not withhold from me your name nor your identity, for you could be such a person that I would abandon my foolish passion out of respect for you or you could be such a person that I would in no way abandon it. It is much better to die quickly than to live a long time and languish in pain such as I have recently begun to endure, for there is no pain which is equal to it."

"Certainly," said the one with the two swords, "I will hide nothing from you which you have asked of me. My baptismal name is Balain, but they have recently started calling me the Knight with the Two Swords."

And when he heard this news, he raised his hand and said:

"Here, my lord, is the sword. I shall give it back to you. And I will from now on do nothing which you might be angry about. I know that you are such a good knight that you will keep to yourself the things you have promised me you would, if a man's good faith has anything to do with it. Know that I know you much better than you think. You are the one who at the court of King Arthur freed the damsel from the sword which she was carrying which no one there but you could do."

And he said that he was truly the one. "But now I beg you to tell me your circumstances."

"I will tell you willingly," said he, "because of the agreement between us."

The one with the two swords said:

"Don't in any way be anxious about the agreement, for I will acquit myself of my obligations, if God please, in such a way that you will be happy and joyful about it."

And then the knight began to tell the tale:

"Sir Balain," said he, "I am a knight born in this country and extracted from vassals and lowly folk. But through my own merit, thank God, I have done so many things that now I am a knight, and I have conquered a great deal of territory and many domains and three beautiful and rich castles that are nearby, which I have won from the Duke of Harneil, whose land borders mine in the direction of Sorelois. I have done such things that I am quite thoroughly respected in this country and in others. Through my prowess I have done well enough that the daughter of the duke whom I mentioned to you, the most beautiful damsel that is known of in any land, gave me her love. She assured me of it in such a way that I consider myself very rich and very fortunate. What shall I tell you? I love no earthly thing except her, not myself nor any other, and know well that I could not live without her. If she wished I would die now, and if it pleased her I would live. Thus in every way I am at the mercy of this beautiful girl so that I don't live unless it be through her. Then four days ago I was in a castle near a fortified place where she was staying with her father, and there she was waiting for a message from me which I had sent to her to discover what she commanded of me. She sent me a silken robe and a damsel who had me put the robe on and dressed me in every way like my lady. Then she led me out in that way in front of the ladies and knights of the place to the damsel's chamber, and there I stayed for two days. And when I left, happy and joyful for my good luck, she swore to me that she would take leave in secret of her father and would be today at noon in front of the tower and then she would go away with me so that I could take her as wife as soon as we arrived in any one of my castles. Thus did my lady, my love, the one in the world I love most swear to me. And it is my opinion that she has sworn an oath to me in a treacherous manner! For I have waited for her as long as I was supposed to and longer and she hasn't yet arrived. And this is the thing which puts my heart into such great anguish and into such contemplative thought that I will never again feel happy until I know the reason for her delay, for I know truly that she would have come here unless her father had prevented her and that she could have had no other reason. Now I have told you the truth about my circumstances and why I was pensive. Now I beg you that you keep your bargain and that I be put in possession of her if you can do anything about it."

"Truly," said the one with the two swords, "I will willingly put into it all the effort which I can to make you and the damsel happy, since she loves you so much. But you will have to take me to the castle where she is, because I could very quickly go astray since I don't know what direction it's in."

"You have spoken well," said the other. "I am ready to take you there. Sir, it is not more than six English leagues. We will be there fairly quickly. Now let us mount and let us leave quickly because it will soon be night."

Then both of them mounted and went off through the forest. As the knight who knew the road well led the way, they spoke with each other about many things so that the trip would seem less burdensome to them. They went along until they came out of the forest. The moon was shining quite brightly and was showing them the way quite clearly. And when they had gone along through the forest for about a league they came down into a deep valley and saw before them a fortress which was surrounded by deep trenches without water and with stakes and hedges. So they both dismounted and tied their horses to two trees because they didn't want the horses to be heard. The one with the two swords asked his companion:

"Will you stay here?"

"Sir I will not. I will go with you and accompany you to a place in the hedge which I know about where you can get through to my lady."

"I could not ask more," said he.

So they went together the two of them and approached the

hedge until they came to a plank which was laid across the ditch. By means of that plank one could get into the damsel's garden, but they had to either straddle it or put a plank next to it because it was so narrow that passage would be very perilous if there were nothing else to rely on, and because the trench which was underneath was so deep that no one could fall into it without breaking either his leg or his thigh since there was no water in it. When he came to the plank the Knight with the Two Swords asked his companion:

"Is this the way to go?"

"Yes, sir. There is no other for anyone who does not want to pass through the main door."

"By my faith," said he, "although this is quite difficult, I will not hesitate because of this, if God please, but I shall pass across. But now tell me where you think I will find your lover."

"Sir," said he, "the very first door that you find on your right is the door of her chamber."

"And how will I recognize her," said he, "if I get to where she is?"

"Because," said the other, "you can recognize her because she is the blondest thing which I have ever seen, nor will you ever see anyone so blond or with such curly hair."

"You have told me enough," said he. "These are such good signs that I must indeed recognize her if I see her."

"I'm really afraid of this passage," said the other.

"Don't worry," said he, "I will indeed pass over it, if God please."

So he hung his shield around his neck and threw his sword into the garden and he got astride the plank, for that was the only way he could possibly have done it. And he was so well armed that he lacked nothing and he got all the way to the other side. When he set foot on the ground he said to his companion:

"Wait for me here since I will bring you news of what you want to know in a little while if I can."

"God be with you," said the other. "I am quite impatient to see you come back."

So the one with the two swords went off into the garden which was very large and beautiful. The moon was shining beautifully and brightly and it showed him the way quite clearly. He went along this way until he came to the door of the chamber which the other had told him about, and he was very happy because he noticed that the door was open so that the cool of the foliage could penetrate the room. Now he went inside and went as quietly as he could so that his armor wouldn't clatter. And once inside he could see very clearly because there were two candles lighted which were giving off considerable light. He looked up and down through the room, which was quite spacious, until he saw next to a chest a very rich and beautiful bed. Then he went straight in that direction because he thought that he would find the damsel sleeping in it. When he arrived at the bed he didn't find the damsel nor anyone else. He looked up and down until he found at the foot of the bed the damsel's robe and the robe of a man. He didn't know whether it belonged to a knight or to a squire. He was amazed since he thought that some knight was probably having sport with the lady and he said to himself:

"Now I know where they are. They went to lie in the grass outside so that they will be cooler than they would be here. And that's why I found the door of the chamber open. Ah, woman, cursed is he who believed in you! Oh, knight, who have today been so distressed and anguished for the love of her, you love her with a much truer love than she does you. Certainly, if I can do anything about it, never again will you be in such great distress as I saw you today because of her, for I will show you how it is with her disloyalty and treachery."

Then the knight went away very sad and very angry and entered the garden, and he went here and there within the garden until he found the young lady lying under an apple tree on a quilt of vermillion samite. She was holding a knight tightly in her arms and had put a great plenty of grass under their heads which was like a pillow, and they were both sleeping as soundly as though they hadn't slept for an entire month. The knight looked at the girl in the light of the moon and saw that she was very beautiful. Then he looked at the knight that she was embracing and saw that he was very ugly and hideous.

"O God," said he, "what an unseemly pair. It seems to me a great marvel that this girl who is so beautiful has abandoned the knight that I found today who is a handsome knight and carries himself well and is brave as far as I know and has taken this one who is so ugly he wouldn't be worthy of entering a place where my compatriots are. Ah, God, he has really chosen this woman well! And now God help me if I don't cause that man who was so unhappy today to understand clearly. He will see what a great folly it can be to give his heart too completely to a woman."

Then he left there and left them sleeping together, and he went until he came to the place where he had entered and called his companion and said to him:

"Come over here and don't tarry, for I will show you a marvel."

And when he heard this word he was even more worried than he was before, so he came to the plank and got on it and passed over it and when he came to his companion he asked him:

"What are you going to show me?"

"You will see quite well," said he. "Follow along after me and go very quietly so that your friend does not wake up."

And they went into the garden until they came to the place where they were sleeping, and the one with the two swords showed the knight his lady.

"You see here the one that you love so passionately. Now you can see whether or not you were wise, you who wanted to kill yourself because she had deserted you. Now know that it was more a question of the one she is holding so tightly in her arms than it was of you. And he is not as handsome and as dignified as you are."

When the knight saw this thing he was so unhappy that he thought that he was going to lose his mind, and he said:

"Ah, alas, what is it that I see?"

104

And he fell to the ground and the blood ran out of his nose and his mouth and he lay there for a long time fainted dead away. Then the one with the two swords was very unhappy because he had showed him this thing, because he saw then that he had fainted for the pain of it. When the knight came to himself after his fainting spell he said to the one with the two swords:

"Ah, sir, you who have shown me so clearly my great misfortune have killed me. It is certain that if you were unarmed no one would guarantee that I would not kill you as a reward for this news and you would have deserved it well because you have committed the greatest sin that a knight has ever committed, and may God treat you the rest of your life in the same way that I will from now on and you will know how it is for a man who loves truly for love's sake."

Then he drew his sword and raised it on high and struck those who were sleeping so hard that he cut off the head of one and the other in such a way that they couldn't speak a word. And when he had done it he was a little calmer than he was before, but after he realized that he had killed his lover, the thing in the world that he loved the most, he repented of it bitterly and said:

"Ah, alas, what have I done? I who have put to death my lady and my heart with her, the one by whom I lived and from whom all my riches and all my joys came. Ah, alas, has any dishonest man ever committed such a horrible act or such great treason as this? Certainly no one!"

Then he began to wail, sorrow, and swear, and carry on the greatest mourning in the world. And his companion comforted him as much as he could, but he said that he was not in need of being comforted by people because never as long as he lived would he be comforted or be happy. And then the one with the two swords was so sad that he wished that he had never in any way thought that he should show the knight his friend in the circumstance that she was in.

When the knight had carried on in this way for a very long time and when he had continued his mourning until almost daybreak and had done it so much that it was a marvel, he said to the one with the two swords:

"Sir, now you can see what you have accomplished by showing me my great sorrow."

And he took his sword by the grip, struck himself with such great force in the chest that the point appeared in the midst of his back on the other side. And he fell backward and emitted a painful groan and began to give himself up to the anguish and the pain he felt. And his eyes turned in his head and then his soul left his body.

And when the Knight with the Two Swords saw what happened, he said that this was the most extraordinary thing that he had ever seen since the girl had killed herself for the sake of her friend. And he was so amazed by this thing that he didn't know what he should do or say, for if he stayed there and was found there, people would think that it was he who had killed them because he was armed and the others were unarmed and they would raise a cry against him and everyone would assemble and it could only be that he would be punished, whatever might happen. So he left them as they were and went to the plank and passed over it and crossed himself many times over because of what he had seen, and he blamed and condemned himself very much and said that he wished that it could be that this horrible happening had never come to pass or that these people had not come to the sort of deaths which they did.

"And it is true," he said, "that this evil thing has happened more because of cursed fate than anything else, because without any doubt I am the most ill-fated knight that there is. It has indeed been proven here and elsewhere."

Thus he tormented himself about what he had witnessed. He was very pained and angry when he came to his horse and he mounted. It was already after dawn and little birds were singing their morning song and were jumping from tree to tree and carrying on with joy and abandon, as you can often see them do. When he was mounted and got onto the road he rode where chance might take him because he absolutely did not know where he was going. And when he came out of the valley he ran into a squire who was going straight toward the fortress from which he had come. He stopped him and asked him if he was going there.

"Yes, sir," said he. "Why do you ask?"

"Because," said the other, "you will find extraordinary things when you come there and only God knows about them, except me, who have seen them. So that those in the place know the real truth, I will tell you about it and then you will tell them the way I have told you."

And so he told about the knight and the girl and how they were killed first off and how the other knight killed himself afterward when he saw that he had killed his lover. When the squire heard this about this happening he crossed himself more than twenty times and said that he had never in all of his life heard tell of such an amazing thing.

"And do you know," said the knight, "why I have told you this tale? I want it to be written down, because after our deaths when it is told to our descendants it will be very eagerly listened to because it is so unusual."

Now tells the tale that with this they separated from each other and the squire went to the place where the others lay dead and found that people inside had already begun mourning and didn't know how this had happened and were talking to each other about various possibilities. So the squire came before them and told them the entire truth the way the thing had happened and said that a knight who had seen it with his eyes had told it to him. Thus came to pass that adventure which was much spoken of in the country.

And the Knight with the Two Swords who had told it to the squire rode along through the land, now in this direction and now in that, as chance dictated.

One day around the hour of dawn it happened that he approached a castle which was built on a mountain. The castle was protected on its right side by the sea and on the other by a fresh water stream that was broad and swift. So the castle was situated so well in all ways that in the whole country there wasn't a more beautiful nor comely one. When he came within a half a league of the castle he found a large cemetery where there were many graves, old ones and recent ones. At the edge of the cemetery near the castle there was a brand new cross. On this cross there were letters which said:

"Do you hear, O knight errant who are going in search of adventure? I forbid you to go any closer to the castle than this. And know you that they are not at all charitable toward a knight."

When he had read the letters he understood quite well what they said because he was quite literate. Then he began to look at the castle and it seemed very beautiful to him. And then he said to himself God help him if he turned back before he had seen the inside of the castle.

"And it is true," he said, "I would have to look upon myself as a coward and bad fellow if I turned back because of the words that I see written here."

So he went past the cross and went with all haste toward the castle. He had hardly gone very far when he encountered an old, venerable, and grey-haired vassal who said to him as soon as he came near him:

"Sir knight, you have passed the boundary and all you have left to do is to turn around."

"Indeed," said he, "I shall go farther and then I will be further from going back. Even though you are dismayed about it, such is my will."

"Indeed?" said the good man.

So the knight did not turn from his way and thus he went farther along the road. And when he was within three bowshots of the castle he listened and heard a horn blow in the main tower with great force, as though it were a deer or a boar hunt. When he heard it he began to smile and said to himself:

"What is this? I think they're on the hunt."

No sooner had he spoken thus than he saw coming out of the castle from the main door more than a hundred damsels, who came singing and dancing and carrying on with the greatest joy that the stranger knight had ever seen in the world. When he approached them they all cried out as with one voice:

"Welcome, good knight who will through his jousting this day fill all the ladies and damsels of this castle with joy."

He returned their greeting and blessed them all at once and they gathered around him giving evidence of the greatest joy in the world. He was so amazed at the happiness that they were showing all around him that he didn't know what to say about it, and they accompanied him along on the road walking in front of him and behind. When he got near the bridge he saw coming out from inside about twenty knights on big warhorses dressed and equipped very richly, and each one of them greeted him and said:

"Lord, welcome."

He bowed to each of them. The lord of the castle came up to him and led him through the door and the knight asked him:

"Sir knight, I beg of you that you tell me why these young ladies are celebrating around me in such a joyful way."

"Sir, it is because of the joy that they feel looking forward to seeing you joust with the knight from the island tower."

"Indeed!" said he. "And they know that I want to joust?"

"Sir, even if you don't want to joust you have to because such is the custom of this castle, that no strange knight comes here upon whom it is not incumbent to joust with the lord of that tower."

Then he showed him the tower which was in the middle of the island. The island was exceedingly beautiful and pretty and the tower which was built in the middle of it was well constructed. And the one with two swords said to the lord:

"Courtly people never established that custom because it is evil and bad. For when a knight errant comes from lands far away tired and exhausted by long days, do you think that it is as easy for him to fight then as it is for the knight in the tower who does nothing but rest? Certainly even if the wanderer were the best knight in the world, when he fights under such conditions I would not be at all surprised if he were beaten. Know that I do not at all say this thing for myself, for I am neither so worn out nor so exhausted but that it would suit me to fight as much as it would the one who has been resting. I am saying it, however, with reference to the custom which is the worst and the most ugly thing that I have seen for a long time wherever I have been."

"My lord," said the lord of the castle, "that is the way our ancestors established it and it has remained thus until our time, I think."

Thus they went into the castle talking with the girls who were still carrying on great joy as they had done before, until they came to the river and found the boat that the knight was to get onto all ready, sail having been set.

"My lord," said the lord of the castle, "your shield doesn't seem to me to be very sturdy. If it pleases you, I would have another one brought to you which is better."

And the knight said that would be fine with him and so he gave his shield to a youth, and the latter took it and went off with great speed to the castle and brought him another and said to him:

"Here you are, sir, this one it seems to me is much better than yours was."

And he took it and hung it around his neck and got into the boat with his horse all armed in such a way that he lacked nothing. The boatman started the boat off and it began to sail away. Then a virgin ran forward and said to the knight who was already approaching the bank:

"Sir knight, it is through evil fate that you have exchanged your shield. If you had it around your neck you would not die today. Thus your friend would recognize you and you him. But God is sending you this evil fate because you have struck King Pelham out of vengeance and there is not vengeance enough to match the deed. Merlin sends me to tell you this."

When he heard these words, he was very fearful because he knew from whom it came. It made him all the more afraid because Merlin told him that it was vengeance for the bad deed he did by striking down King Pelham. He would have given the whole world, if it had belonged to him, to never have entered the castle, for now fear which had never before been able to enter his heart was his companion. Nonetheless, it reassured him that he felt healthy, rested, strong, agile, and skilled with arms. He thought that it would be better to put everything into it and die, if he had to die, than to do something out of cowardice. It also gave him great comfort that he only had to face that one single knight and he felt himself so skilled and clever with arms that he didn't think that there was a single knight in the world who could kill him, no matter how bad off he was or no matter what unfortunate thing might happen. These thoughts lasted until the boat arrived at the island and he was still thinking very earnestly about what the damsel had said to him. The boatman put the horse out of the boat and said to the knight:

"Sir knight, what are you thinking about? Thinking will do you no good. You must go and join battle."

And he got up quickly and said that he had not been thinking at all about the battle. He passed through the boat, crossed himself as he came out, and checked his arms to see that he lacked nothing and held back his horse as best he could. Then he took his shield and his lance and mounted and looked toward the castle and saw the walls and battlements all covered with ladies and damsels who had climbed up there to see the battle. He cursed them all and all those who were responsible for the castle and all those who established this custom and who maintained it, because it was the most evil and treacherous one that he had ever heard tell of.

"And as the Mother of God counsels me," said he, "if it pleases Her that I escape from this battle alive, I will yet have that castle destroyed and all those who live in it, because it was never the abode of honorable people."

The tale tells that then the knight spoke to himself thus and he was impatient to join the battle because he couldn't escape it. He had hardly got there when he saw a knight come out of the tower very well armed in red armor; his shield was vermillion and so was his lance and all of his armor, but his horse was whiter than snow. And he came out of there slowly and he was so well armed that he was lacking nothing that a knight should have. And when he saw the one with the two swords he turned his horse's head and held up his shield which was very beautiful and well made, and when the one with the two swords saw him he thought of his brother who always armed himself to joust more beautifully and better than anyone knew how to do. In such a way his heart was telling him the true news of his brother because now as soon as he saw this man he remembered him, and his heart was indeed telling the truth because this one was his brother, and they would have quickly recognized each other if he hadn't exchanged armor. In such a manner the brother and the twin faced each other as mortal enemies. Like driven beasts they came together at such a speed as fast as the horses could go, lances lowered, and struck each other with such force that they pierced each other's shields and broke the blades of their weapons, but the coats of mail were so strong and held so well that they couldn't even break one link. They struck with such great force that their lances flew into pieces and then they struck each other with their bodies and their shields so hard that they both fell to the ground, stunned and senseless, and neither could get up for quite a while, so they lay there quietly as though they were dead. After a while the one from the tower got up because he was less stunned by the fall than his brother was, and he put his hand on his sword like one who is quick and agile and got ready to attack his brother. When the other saw him coming he didn't feel safe and he was afraid of dying, so he got up more quickly than anyone who had ever been knocked down and stunned and put his hand on his sword, put his shield over his head, and his brother who was striking from above gave him such a heavy blow that he broke off a great piece of the bottom of the shield and it rolled down the hill, and then his blade went further down and cut five hundred links off the end of the body armor. The one with the two swords didn't hesitate a moment but gave a great blow in the midst of his helmet which was exposed, and the helmet was so hard that it prevented the sword from entering into it more than an inch but the other one was made dizzy from the force of the blow.

Then the two brothers began between them a great and amazing battle. They ran after each other up and down and were both full of great strength and pride, and each one was so full of chivalrous spirit that he in no way disrespected the other. Nevertheless, they respected each other and this was amazing. They struck each other with such great force and received such great blows that each one knew that the other one was not an apprentice at this trade. For that reason neither one of them was imprudent about striking blows, and so they watched each other carefully, and each one covered himself as best he could and didn't strike at all as often as he might have. However, if the knight with the Two Swords had felt himself to be as strong as he was in the beginning, he would in no way have been afraid of his companion, but he had been wounded and shaken up by the rough fall that he had taken in the beginning, and because of this he covered himself more and waited until he came toward the end. His brother, who was younger than he and more rested, rained upon him great and heavy blows and harassed him to a great extent, and the Knight with the Two Swords did not spare the other a bit and gave him such great blows that anyone would be hard put to stand them.

The first assault lasted so long that neither one seemed as though he could get his breath back. Neither one of them was in any way losing his skill, although their helmets were crushed and mangled and their surplices torn, their shields were punctured, cut, and fragmented both at the top and bottom, their coats of mail were unraveled, torn, and shattered, and the bodies of the men were mutilated, cut, and wounded so severely that their blood ran over several leagues. And things were in such a state now as a result of these sharp swords that as healthy as they were each had some seven wounds in the body of which another man might think he might well die. And the place where they were fighting was covered with blood and links from their coats of mail and pieces of the covering from their shields.

113

Notwithstanding the great hate that they bore for each other, they were obliged to rest whether they wanted to or not, because in spite of themselves they had to get their breath back. Therefore they separated and put their shields in front of them and leaned on them and neither one of them spoke a word. The one looked at the other and they were both amazed. The one from the tower, because he had found such a good knight, for he didn't think that in all the realm of Logres there was a knight who could hold so long in battle as this one had. Because of the blows that he had given him he thought he could indeed have killed the biggest giant in the world. And for this reason each one respected the other so much that they could not respect each other more.

When they had admired each other for awhile and rested and gotten their breath back, the Knight with the Two Swords was first to pick up his shield and sword, and the other did the same. Then they began again an assault so deadly and perilous that no one saw it without being sorry, because they knew what good knights they were. If they had wounded and battered each other before, this time it was worse because their mail already having been broken and torn and their shields sliced up so that they were worth almost nothing, they were striking each other on bare flesh but not with great strength, because they couldn't, since they had already lost all of their vitality and strength. And if they had been as strong as they were at the beginning, the battle would have soon been over because they were practically disarmed, but they didn't have enough strength left to wound each other very seriously, as they had already lost so much strength and vitality that they could hardly hold up their shields and their swords. And this was no great marvel because they had attacked each other with sharp swords striking this way and that way, so that there wasn't anybody who didn't have at least four mortal wounds either on the head or the body. This was the thing which caused them to abandon the battle.

The battle between the two brothers lasted so long in the manner of which I have told you that they could no longer stand it. And the first to withdraw from the battle was the one from the tower, and at the place where he withdrew he turned around, almost unable to stand up or hold his sword and said to his brother:

"Ah, sir knight, you have killed me, but you can't say that you've beaten me."

And the one with the two swords answered:

"Sir knight, at the same time I'll tell you that you have killed me without any hope of salvation but you haven't beaten me. And it's a shame that you're going to die because certainly you are the best knight that I have ever encountered, and I have encountered many in my travels and beaten many. But after all I must give you the praise and the credit for being the most extraordinary of all. But you can say well that it is unfortunate that you deserve this praise that I am giving you because you are dead because of it. I can moreover say that it is indeed unfortunate that I ever saw you because your strength has killed me. But for the sake of God, though I have come to my end, tell me, if you please, your name so that I might know who killed me."

"Certainly," said he, "I will tell you willingly. Know that my name is Balaan and I'm the brother of the best knight who is now in the world, who is the Knight with the Two Swords. He will be very sad about my death when he learns about it."

When the latter heard that it was his brother before him, he was so sad that he fainted from the anguish that he felt in his heart and fell over backward. And the other one who was watching him thought he was dead and dragged himself up to him because he didn't have enough strength to go there standing up. He undid the other's helmet and took it off his head and opened the facepiece and found that he had three wounds on his head so wide and so deep that a physician's skill would have been useless, because they were too deadly. He looked for a long time but couldn't recognize him because his face was so covered with blood and sweat and his eyes were closed and swollen and his mouth full of dirt and bloody foam. When he recovered from his swoon he said:

"Ah, fair brother, what a disaster this is! I am the one with the two swords of whom you speak who has killed you, and cursèd fate has been so powerful that you have killed me too. Damned be the custom of this castle and damned be all they who are in it because we are now dead before our time."

When the other understood that this was his brother, his pain was great and he answered:

"Sir, because I have killed you by mistake no one can blame me nor you either because you couldn't have recognized me any more than I you. But without any doubt we can say in truth that no more cursèd fate has ever befallen two brothers than it has us. Nevertheless, it should be a great comfort to us that we have found each other before dying, for just as our souls came out of one vessel, so will they be put back into one vessel in this very place where we are now so that after our deaths gentlemen and good knights can see us, and they will feel sorry for the cursèd fate we suffered for the sake of good chivalry and because of the noble deeds they will have heard tell about us."

And then both of them began to cry tenderly and said together:

"O God, why have you allowed such a great tragedy and such evil fortune to befall us?"

While they were thus lamenting their death and their bad luck, along came a lady of a certain age who was the lady of the castle, of the tower, and of the country all around. This lady remained so closely confined within the tower on the island that she never left it, nor did she have in her company but six manservants and six maids who served her all the time, and only seven knights. She had originally been confined in this way by a knight who had no confidence in her, and when he had closed her up there she asked him:

"Sir, why have you put me here?"

"Because," said he, "I want to be sure that no one comes to you except me."

"Then," said she, "you have no confidence in me."

"That's right," said he.

"Well I have even less confidence in you," said the lady.

"I will do," said he, "whatever you command me and then you will no longer doubt me."

"Swear it to me," she said, and he very speedily swore it to her. "Now," she said, "am I reassured because you have sworn to me that never again as long as I live will you leave this tower. Thus you will keep me company both night and day."

And he who was enamoured of her said that he was indeed willing to do it. Thus the knight remained in the tower with the lady. When they had lived there for half a year, he was very much annoyed that he had abandoned the way of arms which he was accustomed to follow, and he caused horses to be brought from the castle and he had his people come from the castle and he had them swear by the saints that never a wandering knight would pass by the castle unless he were made to come to the island to fight with him. And if he found anyone who could beat him at arms and defeat him, he would be willing to be killed by him and to leave the lady to him. And he wanted things to be arranged in such a way that never a knight would leave the island unless he were dead, and he caused everyone in the city to swear that they would maintain it this way after his death.

When the lady came to the knights she saw them so dilapidated and wounded she was very afraid and Balaan said to her:

"Ah, lady, for the sake of God, grant me a boon which will in no way grieve you."

She granted it quite willingly and he thanked her very much. Then he said to her:

"Lady, you have granted to me that in this little spot of ground where we are now lying you will have our bodies deposited beautifully and honorably after we have died and in such a way that the one will be with the other in one grave. And do you know, lady, why I am asking you that we be put in one coffin? Because we came from one vessel that was the belly of our mother, because know you now that this is my twin brother and I am his."

When the lady heard this she was very sad because she saw that they were both excellent knights and so she granted it willingly and cried out of pity. Then she called to the people of her household who were gathered in the doorway of the tower and they came quickly. She commanded that they disarm the knights and carry them to the tower and make them as comfortable as possible. So they disarmed them right away.

And when the one with the two swords was disarmed, he said to the lady, very quietly:

"Lady, don't have me moved from here but bring me a priest and let him bring with him my Saviour for I am dying."

And the other brother asked the same thing. So the lady called the seamen who were on the other bank and told them that they should go to look for the priest so that he could give the sacraments to these two knights who were dying. And they did everything that the lady commanded them right away. So the priest came over to the island all equipped with the things that the knights asked for. And when they had heard the sacraments as any Christian knight should, and they had begged their Saviour for mercy for their sins and their evil deeds, they said to the lady:

"Lady, remember to do for us as you have sworn; to have us buried in this very spot."

And she answered them, crying all the while, that this oath to them would indeed be kept.

After this the two brothers lost the ability to speak nor could they hear another word spoken. They remained alive until the hour of vespers and then died, the youngest first and the eldest next. All the people of the castle came over to the island to see this marvel, and when they knew that they were brothers they said that this was a great tragedy that two such noble men had killed each other. They took a tombstone, the richest they could find in the country, and put it in the spot and both of them in the same place where they had died and had written the name of the youngest upon it upon the right hand side at the bottom of the stone. But for the other one they didn't know what to do because they didn't know his name. Then they asked each other and nobody knew how to call his companion. Then Merlin appeared among them and said to them:

"Let this thing be, because it is no longer your affair. You have done well what was your responsibility."

They all looked to see who it was who was speaking with so much assurance. And he went right up to the stone where the two brothers were interred and began to write on the very stone letters which said:

"Here lies Balain, the Knight with the Two Swords, who struck with the Vengeful Lance the Dolorous Stroke because of which the realm of Listinois was delivered into pain and desolation."

When Merlin had done this he stayed on the island for a little more than a month and cast there various spells. Next to the tomb he constructed a bed that was so strange that no one could sleep in it without losing his mind and his memory in such a manner that he couldn't remember anything which he had done before he came to the island. And this spell lasted until Lancelot, son of the King Ban de Benoic, came there, and then the spell of this bed was broken, not by Lancelot but by a ring which he was wearing which broke all enchantments. This ring had been given to him by the Lady of the Lake, as the great story of Lancelot tells it, that same story which must be omitted from my book, not because it doesn't belong there or that it doesn't have anything to do with it, but because it is better that the three parts of my book be equal, one as long as the other. And if I added that long story, the middle part of my book would be three times as long as the other two. For this reason it is best for me to leave aside this great story which tells the deeds of Lancelot and of his birth, and I want to tell the nine branches of his extraction as it is told by the High Book of the Holy Grail, nor will I tell anything that I must not, thus I will tell a great deal less than I find written in the Latin story. I beg my lord Helye, who was my companion in arms both in youth and in old age, that for love of me and in order to relieve me a bit from this great labor he undertake to recount as I will tell it a little story which belongs in my book, and this branch will be called the Contes del Brait, which is marvelously delectable to hear and to tell. I wouldn't ask him to do this if I thought the book was too long, but for this reason I will ask him to do it, and I know that he is so wise and so subtle that he will be able to tell it all if he wants to make a little effort. I beg him to do so.[16]

But now at this point I will leave off my request because, if God be pleased, I hope he will do as I ask, and I will come back to tell a part of what Merlin did on the island.

When Merlin had caused the bed to be constructed and had done other marvelous things which I cannot tell you here because you will be very bored with the story because there were so many things that happened, he took the sword which Balain had brought there and took off the grip and put another one on it and when he put it there he said to the knight who was with him:

"Now see if you can grasp this grip."

And he tried and he failed and Merlin began to laugh and then he asked him what he was laughing about.

"I am laughing," said Merlin, "because you thought you could take hold of it."

"Why?" said he. "Would it have been such a great marvel if I had taken hold of it?"

"Indeed it would," said Merlin, "because there is no knight alive now in the world who could take hold of it."

"And will there ever come," said the knight, "to this isle a man who will be able to get hold of it?"

"Yes," said Merlin, "one only, and he will have for name Lancelot and he will take the sword away and will kill with it the knight in the world whom he loves the most."

And after this he wrote on the grip letters which said: "By this

16. The reader who is interested in pursuing the clues presented in this passage about composition, is directed to two books: Fanni Bogdanow, *The Romance of the Grail* (Manchester: Manchester University Press, 1960); and C. E. Pickford, *L'Evolution des romans Arthuriens en prose* (Paris: Nizet, 1960).

sword Gawain shall die." And these letters which he wrote there would be found later by Gahariet, the brother of Gawain, and when he saw them and understood them he would think this was all a story and a lie, but then Lancelot would kill Gawain with it and after his death Gahariet, as the true tale tells it.

COLOPHON

THIS TEXT was composed in Monophoto Bembo by
Joh. Enschedé en Zonen, Haarlem, Holland,
whose staff also created the lino cut
design printed on the covers.
The book was printed by offset lithography and bound
in the United States by *Edwards Brothers, Incorporated*.
Production was coordinated by *Elizabeth G. Stout*
of the staff of Northwestern University Press.